Corey Fah Does Social Mobility

Also by Isabel Waidner

FICTION

Sterling Karat Gold
We Are Made of Diamond Stuff
Gaudy Bauble

AS EDITOR

Liberating the Canon:
An Anthology of Innovative Literature

Corey Fah Does Social Mobility

A Novel

Isabel Waidner

GRAYWOLF PRESS

First published by Hamish Hamilton, a division of Penguin Random House UK, London

This publication is made possible, in part, by the voters of Minnesota through a Minnesota State Arts Board Operating Support grant, thanks to a legislative appropriation from the arts and cultural heritage fund. Significant support has also been provided by other generous contributions from foundations, corporations, and individuals. To these organizations and individuals we offer our heartfelt thanks.

MINNESOTA
STATE ARTS BOARD

CLEAN
WATER
LAND &
LEGACY
AMENDMENT

Published by Graywolf Press
212 Third Avenue North, Suite 485
Minneapolis, Minnesota 55401

www.graywolfpress.org

Published in the United States of America

ISBN 978-1-64445- 269-1 (paperback)
ISBN 978-1-64445-270-7 (ebook)

2 4 6 8 9 7 5 3 1
First Graywolf Printing, 2024

Library of Congress Control Number: 2023939964

Cover design: Kapo Ng

'Faster! Faster, Bambi! Don't look back!'

—Bambi's unnamed mother, 1942

I

Corey Fah does social mobility, see how that goes.

I found myself at Koszmar Circus, beneath the old band-stand's prominent, pyramid-shaped roof, contemplating a UFO. When I say UFO I don't mean spaceship. I mean it in the literal sense, Unidentified Flying Object. Circa half a metre tall, it hovered directly in my eyeline. It radiated neon beige, what a concept. I just stood there, one hand on my head, the other on my hip, considering the likelihood.

Was still thinking on it, still processing, when I noticed someone or something moving behind me. I turned around and saw it was Bambi. When I say Bambi I mean Bambi, but not as we know him. On top of his famously unsteady legs, he had four spider's legs, grand total was eight. Besides, he had multiple sets of eyes, like that seraph-filtered kitty on Instagram, or most common spiders: pavouk, in one Euro language. The fawn looked at me, batting four sets of lashes, giving disarming smile. Off he went, hustling around the bandstand, rattling the local blue tits to the core.

My modus operandi was dissociation and tonight was no exception. This was a deer-in-headlights situation, and by deer I mean myself, not Bambi Pavok. I was at a loss what to do, especially about the task I'd been sent to carry out.

Did I say, I'd won a mad prize, likely by mistake. 'The Award for the Fictionalisation of Social Evils goes to—.' Chair of the judging committee saying my name, Corey Fah. That'd been at the online winner announcement I'd attended with Drew Szumski, my soulmate and partner, earlier tonight at home in our flat on Sociální Estate. Drew going, shut the front door! Wtf!

I'd missed much of what had followed the announcement. I'd just sat there in my white Fruit-of-the-Loom type charity shop t-shirt and watched myself on the livestream. I'd worn grey cotton joggers, t-shirt tucked in, a detail wasted on camera, of course. Black brogues, I'd got them involved. I was fairly certain, though, that in the after-session to the public announcement the prize coordinator had asked me to go Koszmar Circus and collect the physical representation of the cultural capital I'd just acquired. 'Go get your trophy,' she'd said. 'Do it quickly, before the judges change their minds.' I hadn't been sure if she was joking or not.

So I'd told Drew I'd be going. 'What, now?' they'd asked. Would be an hour's walk at a minimum, even if I cut through the little woods just south of estate. No matter, I'd left straight away.

Koszmar Circus was an ornamental mount at the

centre of a social housing estate in the east of the international capital. Surrounded by thirteen-storey-high concrete apartment blocks, it felt fenced in. Blackthorn, hawthorn and elder bushes grew in concentric flower beds between street level and the first tier, and again, between the first and second tiers. Historical bandstand on top. Problem was, I couldn't see any trophy. Just the UFO and Bambi Pavok. Pampas grass in mid-distance. Was I in the wrong place, I wondered. Had I misunderstood the instructions. Detail had, I want to say, not been forthcoming. More like, withheld. 'It'll be self-explanatory,' the prize coordinator had said. The assumption had been that a winner would know how to collect. That prize culture etiquette, its unwritten rules and regulations, would be second nature to them. But I didn't, know how to collect; and they weren't, second nature to me. I'd not won an award before, and neither had anybody I knew.

A lot going on for me at this juncture, and that was without Bambi Pavok feeling his feelings over there. He'd seemed fine before, but now he was lying against the bandstand's historical railing, head buried in two sets of front legs at least. He was having tears. I hadn't known, but in 1942, Bambi Pavok had lost his mother to Man, apparently——.

Back in his native Forest, death had arrived in the shape of a person with a legalised gun, firing shots in a blinding snowstorm. Bambi Pavok and his mother had run, fast as they could, dodging bullets. 'Faster, Bambi Pavok! Don't look back! Keep running!' Mother had called.

So Bambi Pavok ran for his life. Always looking ahead, he made it into the safety of the single-parent family hideout. 'We made it, Mother!' he exclaimed. The relief was short-lived. When Bambi Pavok turned around, he saw that his mother hadn't, in fact, made it. She'd fallen behind. 'Mother?' No answer.

Despite the danger, Bambi Pavok went back outside to look for her. Snow fell thicker now. 'Mooother!' Nothing. Tentatively at first, Bambi Pavok ventured deeper into the woodland, all the time calling, 'Mother, where are you!' He bounded from tree to tree, stopping, calling, and cocking his ears. Still no response. Bambi Pavok picked up the pace, searching a wider territory now. He slalomed round fir trees a hundred times taller than him. He zigzagged through pines. Eventually, he slowed down, calling his mother increasingly unconvincingly. 'Mother——.' Until he stopped.

Oh! Bambi Pavok shot up like a flick knife. The False Widower of the Forest appeared right in front of him – a spider the size of a twelve-pointer stag. 'Your mother can't be with you anymore,' False Widower said – whistled, rather, through the drinking-straw-like device that was his mouth.

Hearing this, Bambi Pavok caved in a little. He got it, mum's dead. He shed one single tear. One. That was it. No floodgates. Not like under the bandstand over there.

'Come,' False Widower said, 'my son.' He turned around and walked off, expecting to be followed. But Bambi Pavok hesitated. He looked back. No mother. No doe. Just snow and foreboding Forest. He had no choice but to follow the False Widower into the white, abominable winter.

Begged the question, what was Bambi Pavok doing here at Koszmar Circus in the east of the international capital, in 2024. After the death of his mother, hadn't he rebuilt his life in the Forest? Why hadn't he aged during the intervening years, eighty-two by my calculation? At least he seemed chirpier now, getting up and playing among the hydrangeas. Suited me, I had urgent matters to see to. A trophy to collect. Where was it——.

As I tried to refocus, the UFO was making its presence felt. Under the bandstand's pyramidal roof, it started to tremble. It was dialling up the neon beige glow, as if it were vying for my attention.

It got Bambi Pavok's. Mouth full of flowers, the latter tilted his head, wondering what the agitation was about. He let go of the dog rose he'd been mauling and came running over. He hurtled right past me, towards an already skittish UFO, jumping up, and snapping at it, yelling, 'bir, bir', and eventually, 'bir-ddd', like the UFO were a bird, freaking it out.

Without warning, the Unidentified Flying Object swung out wide over Koszmar Circus. It hovered for a second, taking bearings of, as far as I was concerned, nevereverland, and took off. Whereas I was left on Earth with Bambi Pavok.

2

Corey Fah and Drew Szumski watch their favourite television show.

Drew Szumski and I lived in a one-bed flat on Sociální Estate, a 1960s social housing estate in the Huàirén part of the capital. Built into slopey terrain, a hundred and fifty flats spread across several four-storey terraces of pale grey brick, all with glass doors leading out onto balconies – patios, even, on the top-floor flats, including ours. Once, a local supermarket and community spaces optimistically had been arranged across the ground floor of one of the terraces. Now out of business, they'd been overtaken by knotweed which the council had given up contending with. The one shop left and thriving was the butcher's who'd set up in the former GP surgery. Due to its monopoly on estate, it had expanded into stationery, basic toiletries and portable firearms.

This was the afternoon after the winner announcement. I never slept in, but today I did. Only reason I got up when I did was, *St Orton Gets to the Bottom of It* was about to come on, Drew's favourite tv show. It was the one programme we still watched together on television in real time, almost ritualistically. Three pm slot above anything else, was the idea. Life could wait half an hour.

'*Gets to* about to come on,' I said, walking into the living room.

'Those your clothes from last night?'

Drew had a point. I hadn't noticed.

They switched on the tv, TBC One. We settled on the sofa we'd retrieved from a neighbour who'd disappeared last year and whose flat had stood empty since. Council didn't let out flats that became vacant anymore, which made us suspect they'd evict the remaining tenants including us sooner or later. Milky sun fell through grimy windows onto lino flooring, competing with the televised image.

'You ok?' Drew asked, scrutinising me.

'Later,' I said, nodding towards the tv. I just wanted to sit for a while without having to explain myself.

The show's theme tune came on, dah-deedle-dum oh oh oh – some Austrian pop song in a minor key with vaguely sinister undertones. The tune accompanied a visual making us, the viewers, feel like we were racing through a black hole or tunnel, an abstract burrowing surrounded by warped darkness. Just as we hurtled towards a light, the screen went dirty pink top to bottom, and the title, *St Orton Gets to the Bottom of It*, came on in maroon capital letters. Everything in the sequence pulled against everything else: the slow tune against the pacey visual, and the bottom-oriented title against the upwards momentum of the animation. Maroon on dirty pink was neat, though, Drew would say circa twice weekly. Two colours that for all intents and purposes should clash, but that complemented each other, not entirely, no, but compellingly. Was like visual A S M R for Drew. Besides, it reminded them of our relationship. Joking, not joking.

Drew had been named after the child actress Drew Barrymore, and they'd kept the name, primarily because of its nonbinary potential. They cried often and easily, usually on behalf of someone else. A descendant of first-generation immigrants, they had love for anything vulnerable and a pronounced sense of injustice. Dark blond or light brown hair, what's the difference, a little longer these days as was the fashion. Light brown eyes like something sylvan, like life in the undergrowth or beneath the earth. They'd grown up in the capital, though. Keep-off-the-grass sign outside their estate. No way of knowing how they'd react to Bambi Pavok, is my point.

Cut to a basic talk show set-up. The white working-class presenter, Sean St Orton, made a habit of appearing in boxing shorts only, purple-grey zigzag print, revealing his subtle musculature and a tattoo of a swallow across his lower abdomen covering an appendectomy scar. Other than that, he wore sports socks and either Air Jordans or Aldi sliders – the latter today. In his mid-forties – there were controversies, perhaps cultivated, over his exact age – Sean had an irreverent, simultaneously modest and overconfident demeanour that Drew and the rest of his fans adored. Thing kept everyone watching, though, was Sean's personal investment in his project, his stubborn determination to get to the bottom of 'it', that is, irregularities in the spatiotemporal continuum, how they worked and impacted on people's lives.

That's what Drew said the appeal was, anyway. Was as riveting as it was frustrating seeing someone, Sean, so driven, so bloody-mindedly pursuing a personal project that none of us had thought was our concern until he'd made it just that. For the longest time, whenever Drew'd talked about 'bloody-mindedness', 'personal project', or anything to that effect, I'd worried that indirectly they'd been commenting on the way I'd been going about my writing, and not *St Orton Gets to the Bottom of It* at all. But when I'd shared my anxieties, Drew had replied, 'Not everything is about you, Corey. I have my own interiority.'

Anyway, Sean purported he used to be shit-hot playwright in the 1960s. He'd gone by a different name then, I forget, not sure I ever knew. Said he'd escaped a domestic violence situation in '67, his homosexual lover coming for him in the studio flat the couple had shared on Kalapács Road, coincidentally in the Huàirén borough, not far from estate. He'd got out by disappearing through what he'd termed a červí díra – a space-and-time-defying passageway, a transdimensional wormhole – that earlier that year had opened up in his flat inexplicably, on the floor by his bed. He'd gone down it, and after a short trip, he'd ended up here – 'here' referring to this timeline a decade ago, 2014, somewhere in the capital, where exactly was one of the many, many details he'd forgotten but hoped to recover. In the intervening years, he'd come up with a working theory involving four- or five-dimensional shortcuts connecting disparate points in space-time – as I said, červí díry. What's more, he'd reinvented himself as a tv personality debating self-same. He'd always had charisma, which had stood him in good stead in the past.

Live on tv, Sean sat in one of two grey leather swivel chairs. Behind him, the black burrowing of the title sequence continued to run, turning into deep pink and maroon intermittently.

'He looks tired,' Drew commented. Bad-tempered, even.

Today's guest, one Mallory, or Malachi, Hölderlin from Florida Rot, the swampy part of town, sat on the other chair. The twenty-year-old's brown hair was held up in a tenuous bun. A surplus of hairpins and clips on the sides and top of her head contributed to her looking, I don't know, vexed, or vulnerable, what was it about her. Her black t-shirt had a gothic print on it, and was complemented by black shorts, nylon tights and DM shoes. She had a pet rabbit on her lap, agitating.

'Do you have anyone in the audience, Malachi? Parents? A friend?' Sean asked.

No. Malachi didn't have any friends. Just her bunny. He'd been her confidant throughout secondary school and her first year of uni still. At present, she could barely control him, he was fidgeting so hard. He was thumping her lap with the long part of his hind leg. Thump-thump-thump-thump.

'Ok, no friends, no problem. So Malachi. Why did you come on the show,' Sean asked. 'What do you want out of this.' He tended to stick to a series of standard questions before going off on tangents, feeling his way through the interview, creeping into his guest's psyche, all the while getting closer to the bottom of whatever 'it' might turn out to be that day. Made for compelling viewing.

Accordingly, Drew leant forward. They had a feeling this was going to be good.

Simple, Malachi said. She wanted to know what had happened to her bunny. Apparently, he had gone, like, *gone*, from his indoor home, a cage, three weeks ago. Eleven days later, he'd returned, changed. She'd suspected červí díra at once.

Malachi'd reckoned with spatiotemporal abnor-

malities in her home for some time. Way bunny had
come into her life in the first place had been unusual.
One day, circa a decade ago, Malachi herself had been,
what, ten, he'd sat under the washbasin, one-toothed
baby, shivering on the icy white bathroom tiles. He'd
come out of nowhere, pine needles stuck in his fur. The
sharp parts of a conifer under his tongue. Malachi had
thought that her mother had put him there, but had she.
'She said she didn't, but she lies a lot.' Further, Malachi
had located a grey fluff ball right by the sink. Bunny fur.
At the time, she hadn't known what to make of it.
Hadn't been until she'd got into *St Orton Gets to the
Bottom of It* some years later that she'd put two and two
together, and realised that the drain of her washbasin,
and she was not saying this lightly, was červí díra. How
else could she explain the rabbit's unlikely appearance
on her bathroom floor years ago? Did Malachi say, she
was a fan of the show?

Anyway, chances were, if bunny'd gone down
that route once, he'd done it again. Three weeks ago,
he'd dived into the enamel wormhole, Malachi was certain of it. She hadn't a clue where he'd gone. But, like
she said, eleven days later, he'd been back in his cage.
Same as before, but with a personality disorder. Displayed strange behaviour.

'The thumping?' Sean guessed.

'No, he's always done that. Other stuff. Adult

stuff. I can't say on tv.' Besides, he'd been wet through and through, and he'd smelled, y'know, iron-y. Know when you bite your tongue and draw blood? Malachi hadn't been able to get the smell out of the rabbit, not with shampoo, nor detergent. Repeat washing hadn't done anything, apart from, he'd developed contact dermatitis. Inflamed patches, see there? And there? Ultimately, she wanted to fix . . . *this*. Could Sean help? Malachi held her bunny up to the light, camera closing in. The animal moved his legs hectically, all four of them now, and squealed.

A purposeful camera swipe across the forty-seater grandstand facing the host and his guest revealed unconcealed expressions of distaste from the studio audience. Exhilaration, too. People were happy to feel something, anything, in relation to a problem that wasn't theirs.

Sean looked at the rabbit. Well, well. Washbasin, huh? Červí díra? A mocking tone had entered into his questioning lately that didn't serve him or the show very well. Made him sound like he disrespected his guests. I watched Drew's brow furrow.

'Can you confirm——. When did the rabbit arrive in your life?' Sean asked.

'2014. Ten years ago.'

Drew sat up again, anticipating. Normally, Sean would be all over a mention of 2014, a prolific year for červí díra activity to his mind. But today, even '14 fell flat.

Sean told Malachi outright that, if he were to venture a guess, the pet rabbit's recent absence and change of behaviour had nothing to do with spatiotemporal irregularities at all, but rather with the animal's advanced age. Like people, rabbits became recalcitrant as they got on. Less tolerant of their constraints. 'Did you search the flat? Really search it? Could it be he hid behind the sofa for a while? Got bored and came back?' Sean preferred not to comment on bunny's manifestation in Malachi's bathroom as a baby. Who goes Florida Rot anyway, rough part of town. Miry.

Taken aback by Sean's quick dismissal and apparent indifference, Drew grabbed my hand. Ditto the studio audience, they all held onto each other's hands. What was going on—.

'You're not gonna come round and investigate the washbasin?' Malachi asked, stunned.

Not at all. Ten minutes into the show, and Sean was done. He called it there and then: neither Malachi Hölderlin nor her červí díra was the real deal. As for her pet rabbit — waste of Sean's time. Studio audience went, Wow. Wtf. On cue, a variation on the theme tune came on in yet another minor key. The presenter turned away from his guest and viewers at home, and turned inwards. A camera close-up captured a twitch by the side of his eye, a barely noticeable and what felt like deeply private response. This wasn't remarkable in itself: the show often ended in disappointment, if not Sean's, then the guest's — but not usually until all lines of enquiry had been exhausted, which tended to be a minute or two before the end of the regular half-hour programme slot.

Disappointment because, they never were, the real deal. Guests' stories always failed to comply with the unspecified set of criteria that Sean had established and that defined a bona fide červí díra experience in his opinion. In the four years the show had been running, there had been two maybes. Everything else, definite nos. Hadn't stopped Sean from taking himself and his guests seriously, nor from chasing červí díry compulsively. If anything, all those false alarms had led Sean and his fans to deduce that space-and-time-defying passageways were extraordinarily rare.

Twenty minutes' running time left, Drew and I watched Malachi Hölderlin put her bunny under her arm and lean forward in her chair. 'It's ok, Seany,' she said, consoling the older, more powerful, host. 'It's ok, you know.' With no response forthcoming, Malachi began to feel a little self-conscious. She got up from her chair, hesitated, then hurried off set. Whereas he who'd set the rules of engagement, whose name was in the title, just sat there distraught, man-child in boxing shorts. The shot expanded, revealing the animated červí díra behind him that, right now, Sean probably wished would take him away. We all did.

Has to be said that out of the two of us, Drew was the original fan of the show. I'd got onto the St Orton bandwagon because of Drew. Drew's commitment was contagious, and besides, once you'd watched a couple of times, it was easy to go with the flow. If I had any doubts re the host, his credibility, or the format, likely exploitative, and that's before Sean's recent turn to cynicism, I'd put them to one side. Drew took everything St Orton said at face value and in good faith, and I, having had trust issues from young, loved them for it.

In a recurring motif, a fan favourite at that, Sean started what might be described as 'rallying', following the let-down. He got it together enough to deliver a semi-uplifting ending, a casual salute, albeit way prematurely. He heaved himself up from his chair and addressed the studio audience and us at home directly. Tomorrow was another day, Sean said, another show. Another opportunity for him, for us, to get to the bottom of another guest's červí-díra-related predicament. Tune in at three pm! Weekdays.

Someone in the control room made the executive decision to run the closing credits fifteen minutes early – what else were they going to do. A continuity voiceover announced an unscheduled rerun of a TBC mini reportage on women drivers in Bahrain. Drew got up, let the telly run for the glint, but lowered the volume.

'He didn't even try,' they said, apropos of Sean's performance today. It hadn't seemed right. *Sean* hadn't seemed right, Drew felt.

'Anyway. Let's have a look at this,' they said, changing the topic. They picked up a plastic bag from estate butcher's which they'd parked by the side of the sofa. Grinning, they pulled out a selection of today's newspapers – *Gazeta Wyborcza*, the *Guardian*, the *New York Times*, *Al Jazeera* print edition – all of which were reporting that I, Corey Fah, 40, had won the Award for the Fictionalisation of Social Evils last night. 'Look here, Corey, and here.' Drew located my name on pages twenty-three, sixteen, thirty-seven and, once, four of the various broadsheets. Headlines ranged from UNKNOWN FAH WINS £10K PRIZE FOR 'MIND-BENDING' DEBUT NOVEL to BLOGGER TAKES MAJOR LITERARY AWARD. I couldn't help notice the disproportionate number of mentions of the 'inclusion agenda' that the prize had adopted, allegedly. What else, the papers smelled of meat.

'So what happened at Koszmar Circus last night,' Drew asked. 'I didn't hear you come home? Let's see the trophy.'

'I don't have it.'

'What you mean, you don't have it.'

'It wasn't there.'

Birds in the tree outside the window chirping, bir, bir! Birr-d!

'How can it not have been there.'

'It just wasn't.'

'Did you tell Social Evils?'

'Not yet.'

Birrrrrr-ddddd.

My phone went. Was on silent, but the screen lit up.

'Take it,' Drew said. 'Might be them.'

As a rule, I didn't answer calls from unknown numbers.

Drew thought I should email the prize organisers, then. Tell them what had happened, or not happened, as it were, at Koszmar Circus last night.

'About that, Drew——.'

Not now. Drew needed to get ready for their shift. Did I say, they were full-time employed as a translator, or 'interpreter', in various state-funded hospitals across the north and east of the capital. Self-taught entirely, they specialised in several Central European languages including Polish and Czech. Plus, they had a working knowledge of Cantonese. Drew went to have a shower, leaving me to it.

I emailed the Social Evils prize coordinator, inform- ing her that, through no fault of my own, I hadn't been able to collect the trophy. I hoped this could be rectified without too much additional admin. Could the trophy be delivered, for instance, to my home address? I lived locally, Huàirén. I also enquired how soon I could expect to receive the prize money. I had bills to pay, a partner I owed. Neither of us had notable savings, nor familial backing, I thought she should know. Like most working-class people, I assumed, wrongly, the award's value was monetary, rather than in its prestige and social power.

Instant reply. What had seemed to be the issue at Koszmar Circus. They tended not to have any problems.

The trophy wasn't there, I replied.

Oh it was. Neon beige this year. Likes to hover.

Fuck. Fuck fuck fuck fuck. I typed something. Deleted it. Typed something else. No good either. I settled on, It got away.

Prize coordinator was sorry to say that my failure to collect brought with it a whole set of bureaucratic impracticalities. Number one, she wouldn't be able to ID me – a formality usually dealt with in a straightforward video call. Winner, trophy, trophy, winner, united in one livestreamed image, was all the evidence she required to initiate the transfer of funds, for instance.

I have a passport, I replied.

Not acceptable, prize coordinator replied, now cc'ing the literary director of the award. Other potential problems included the wrongful seizure of the trophy by an unauthorised member of the public. I hadn't left it unsupervised, had I? What if someone took it? What if a finders-keepers type person video-called her with the trophy, claiming it as their own and requesting the prize money?

You'd notice it wasn't me? I replied. Common sense? We met online several times, most recently during last night's winner announcement. Plenty of photos and footage of me going round, too, including a reaction video your comms team posted less than twenty-four hours ago. Surely, you'd be able to tell me apart from an impostor, I pressed send, making my point. Personally, I'd know the prize coordinator's shoulder-length wave with the fringe anywhere, her saucer-sized glasses on a lanyard, and her flouncy blouse with the #DecoloniseLiterature pin. Another one saying 'Ally'. Was it too much to ask she should recognise me in a video call?

You say that, came the reply. But would I. Prize coordinator'd had three emails this morning already from senders impersonating me. PLEASE TRANSFER £10K ASAP, BEST WISHES, COREY FAH. All caps, designed to dazzle the recipient into rash action. In many ways, more credible than my actual emails. More professional-sounding. They'd set up fake PayPal accounts in my name, everything. Look it up, Corey Fah. Literary award fraud is a thing. Recipient, sender and exact amount to be transferred all over the newspapers, an invitation to online scammers. You seem a little naive, if you don't mind me saying. Unversed in the intricacies of award culture. What secondary school did you say you went to, again? Anyway, we need to rearrange trophy collection urgently.

How would it work?

Return to Koszmar Circus. If, and that's *if*, no one else had claimed the trophy, the prize coordinator would attempt to reteleport. Usually, teleportation auto-initiated once, and once only, following the winner announcement. In this case, she'd have to manually override. No guarantee it would work. Come to think of it – it might be better if I sent someone else to collect on my behalf. Someone I could trust, ideally more than myself. Someone competent. My agent?

No agent. It would have to be Drew. I typed, Consider it done. Send.

'Drew, when are you working this week?' No answer. 'Drew?'

I looked around and saw that the bedroom door was wide open. Drew stood by the side of the bed, their back turned to me. They were looking up towards the ceiling, raising their hand high as possible, as if to communicate with someone or something up there. I craned my neck, trying to see what they were seeing, not that I didn't have my suspicions. There he was: Bambi

Pavok hung upside down from the ceiling – a little sinister-looking, yet inexplicably charming. Oh dear, I thought. He'd chosen *not* to stay in the temporary bed I'd made for him late last night, quietly bundling up sweaters and t-shirts, whatever else I'd been able to find, and arranging them beneath my side of Drew's and my bed. Instead, he'd got up before I'd had opportunity to tell anyone, Drew, about him.

To be clear, Bambi Pavok was a significant natural presence. We could smell his damp fur. Dirty footprints all over the floor, up the wall and across the ceiling. With respect to Drew's hand, he showed an interest, but hesitated. Took a tentative step in Drew's direction, then hung back again. Drew didn't move. They didn't say anything, just nodded encouragingly, as in, come here. It's ok. That did it. Wide-eyed, times eight, Bambi Pavok bounded across the ceiling, pushing his face against Drew's hand with affection. 'Baby,' the latter said tenderly. 'Where did *you* come from?'

Baby. Really. They barely called me that anymore. Evidently, my concerns in regard to Drew and their compatibility with the natural world had been misplaced. In fact, they took to Bambi Pavok almost instantly. I couldn't say the same for myself, if I'm honest. At best, I was on the fence.

3

Corey Fah hates on their younger self, but doesn't admit to it.

Watching *Bambi* the animated film has been a rite of passage for generations, introducing the concept of parental death to unsuspecting children arguably prematurely. For millions of us, for whom Bambi figures as *thee* corruptor of childhood naivety, for whom Bambi was the first, Bambi Pavok is the lesser evil in many ways.

Naturally, we accept Bambi Pavok losing his mother much more readily than Bambi losing his. Our collective hearts break for him to a lesser degree and not quite as irredeemably. Bambi Pavok's devastation is an infinitely more palatable proposition for the straightforward reason that, clearly, he's been corrupted all along. He's been othered from the beginning. You can't unspoil Bambi Pavok only to spoil him again more effectively. Even before his mother's death, his life in the Forest was permanent trash fire in 1942. He was caught up in the socioeconomic systems designed to disadvantage and kill-by-stealth the racially othered, the sick and disabled, the working classes, the lower castes, and anyone who, simplistically speaking, wasn't born within a twenty-mile radius. Unlike Bambi, Bambi Pavok had opportunity after opportunity to prepare himself, develop his crisis responses, and ultimately dissociate, deaden himself to a world which kept claiming what has always been its, the world's, never his, Bambi Pavok's. That's why it hurts less. For all intents and purposes, Bambi Pavok's grief should hurt him less than Bambi's grief hurt Bambi. If Bambi Pavok didn't take any of the opportunities that presented themselves, again and again, to get accustomed to earth-shattering loss; if he deliberately and persistently kept opting out of trauma training; if this latest bereavement isn't just one in a never-ending series of bereavements to him, and if, as a result, it doesn't hurt less, then he actually probably deserves what he has coming, psychic destruction.

Thing with Bambi Pavok is that, unlike Bambi, he gives the impression he's able to fend for himself, and he almost certainly is. Matter of fact, he was fending for himself while his mother was still alive. Bambi Pavok's mother was nothing like Bambi's. Bambi Pavok's mother'd had it from the beginning, she'd had it coming, only questions were how and when. Ultimately, a protracted death – by prescription painkillers, long-term unemployment and ever-increasing financial arrears – was cut short by a fatal gunshot wound instantly, perhaps mercifully. But who's to say that a bad life is worse than no life, not me. Never me. Hard to judge Bambi Pavok's mother's mental health or her fitness for raising a child historically, but who throws themselves at a spider wasteman, False Widower of the Forest or not. Who even does that. It's not like he's the Great Prince of the Forest or anything – Bambi's father is. And yet, the False Widower was going round the green hills and valleys as though he owned everything, while she was stuck in her bat-cave with Bambi Pavok, his bastard child.

Enough of the mother. Was just Bambi Pavok now, flying solo. Not even his friends, if he had any, could bring themselves to feel sorry for him, this is why: take the hypothetical scenario of a little friend – a one-toothed rabbit named Fumper, say – responding to Bambi Pavok's ongoing histrionics passing for grief. 'What's so bad,' Fumper might say. 'You're better off without her. Are you gonna live with the False Widower of the Forest, or not? Even if he'll turn out a wasteman eventually, and who says he will, he's still your father, not everyone has one. He live in a palace, isn't he?' Fumper himself of course lived in a hole in the ground with twenty-five family members, so there's that.

Thing about Bambi Pavok is, he doesn't know how good he actually has it. He refuses to count his blessings. He shits on the positives. He was gifted this new lease of life by his father, but judging from the way he was stomping on wild geraniums, putting his heel in and twisting, you'd be forgiven for thinking he was headed straight for the local abattoir, not the False Widower residence at all.

The other thing about Bambi Pavok is, as much as his feelings are lacking sincerity, they tend to run away with him. Remember his shedding one single tear on realising what had happened to his mother? His understated, almost elegant way of carrying himself in the face of indescribable loss? Was a fluke. Was something he copied off Bambi. Bambi Pavok's true inclination is to express his so-called pain through red-faced kicking and screaming. So OTT and affected. There's no self-control, no bodily containment. He wasn't brought up right, is what it is, did his mother teach him anything. There's no 'you smile, the world smiles back at you' discernible effort or basic understanding of karma. Nothing of the sort. On that basis alone, Bambi Pavok will never be Bambi. He'll never elicit the compassion Bambi elicits, not in a million years, not ever-ever.

So how's that going, living with dad.

False Widower was no Great Prince of the Forest, he was liar king, not everyone knew. No palace, for starters, just a souterrain under the maggoty maple tree. For a while, False Widower perpetuated the lie that he was the host of a popular tv show, broadcasting live from a studio in the Forest and all across the Soviet Union, of all places. He was famous in Soviet Union, he'd say, improbably and, pre-internet, unverifiably.

He could move there and ice-bathe in public admiration. Only thing stopping him was, he preferred the anonymity of life in the Forest and, oh, Bambi Pavok, his uncalled dependant. 'What would you say if I moved to Azerbaijan and just left you here,' the False Widower would say to Bambi Pavok on a regular basis. If Bambi Pavok carried on like this, he just might. What else. Another time False Widower said he was fast-food restaurateur. He started walking around the Forest with a clipboard, scouting for potential venues. He also pretended to speak several African and South-East Asian languages, like, Swahili, Yoruba, Khmer and Burmese. Said he could be a professional translator if he wanted to, when all he ever talked was BS. Sometimes, fuck, he went as far as to purport to be a writer, a rhetorician, a polemicist, whose hot takes informed politicians and decision-makers, including the Great Prince of the Forest, original Bambi-father. Why did he do it? Cos he was liar king fucking wasteman with a frustrated sense of entitlement and sadistic leanings. He'd rather believe his own lies than confront his relative insignificance within the ecosystem of the Forest, and, what else, he'd just been handed a Bambi-Pavok-shaped plaything on a platter.

At first, Bambi Pavok believed the lies: the talk show host, disappearing the day in the studio. The restaurateur, planning new ventures. Or the language maverick helping precarious forest animals find their way in life. Bambi Pavok was young and credulous, False Widower grown-up and without any conscience. The former didn't yet know, didn't even consider, that anyone, never mind his own father, could be lying through his teeth, or past his drinking-straw mouthpart, as a matter of course. Not that youth is an excuse – Bambi Pavok should've been way more switched on than he was, he was already three or four. Children grow up quicker in the uncivilised Forest, it's not like round here in the international capital: Fumper basic- ally running an entire household age two and a half, allowing his mother and father to focus on propagation, was the societal norm. But Bambi Pavok isn't Fumper. He is easy to manipulate, is his problem. His relative immaturity and gullibility are further reasons why, ultimately, Bambi Pavok's fate leaves most of us stone- cold and unbothered. We simply don't care what will happen to him, not like we cared about Bambi in that rural cinema in the forties, fifties, sixties and seventies, or on tv in the eighties and nineties, or on YouTube two thousands onwards. Glad to report that, eventually, Bambi Pavok began to suspect that things weren't right. He started asking questions, out loud, like, why you come home from tv studio reeking of vodka. What's 'liar king' in Burmese? Why you come home yelling at me, and why is there never any gas or electricity in the souterrain under the manky maple tree. Bambi Pavok's inquisitive, confrontational manner was like asking for it, needless to say. He started coming into his own as his father's plaything and stress ball, to be squashed, chewed up and pelted, as required.

As far as parents go, False Widower of the Forest was alive, but ultimately that's all that can be said in his favour.

Worth noting that Bambi Pavok's personal situation and emotional state dovetailed with a wider atmosphere of fear and trepidation in the Forest of 1942: a drastic decimation of the local deer population was being recorded at the time and reported across the local media. Deer had been disappearing, Bambi Pavok's and Bambi's mothers representing just two of a staggering number of recent killings and kidnappings. Something was amiss in the Forest and had been for a while. Was it Man? Was there something else going on?

One day, False Widower told Bambi Pavok that a new fast-food restaurant, Frikadellen, Best in Forest, had opened less than a mile away. 'Know what they are, frikadellen?' False Widower asked. 'Meat burgers, Bambi Pavok. Venison, to be exact. They fry little Bambis there twenty-four-seven. That's right, industrial quantities. Adult game, too. Demand far exceeding current supply, what you think about that. Queues going out the door at the opening this weekend.' Hearing this,

Bambi Pavok went weak at the knees, as well as various other joints in his many-segmented legs. Was False Widower lying, as per? Or could it be true—.

Another day, False Widower came home with a burger-size carton. It was pink-brown and said 'Frikadellen, Best in Forest' on it in red lettering. False Widower kept smelling it, going yum, delicious. After hours of taunting, he finally opened the box. There it was, the frikadelle, inside a sliced sesame bun, sunk in on itself by that point. False Widower removed one, two, three cucumber slices, and ate the rest in front of Bambi Pavok. Hm, he said. So tasty.

That's when the nightmares started. Every night Bambi Pavok dreamt, not just of himself as a burger, sausage, or schnitzel with French fries, feeding the wealthier among the Forest's demographics, but of his mother, too. What if she'd ended up in a giant meat grinder, he'd never know. Initial relief felt on waking subsided rapidly as the nightmare that was his waking life imposed itself every day.

No rabbit stew on the menu, a critical distinction which quickly gave rise to a culture of bullying in the Forest. Led by Fumper the rabbit, Bambi 'Mincemeat' Pavok's so-called friends kept ridiculing and harassing him. Because of his psychotic home life, the latter could be a little uncommunicative. He might have developed a speech impediment. In any case, Fumper took pleasure in trying to make him say words, like 'bird', for example. 'Say bird,' Fumper would say. 'Bir,' Bambi Pavok would give it a go. 'Bir-*d*.' '*Birrr*.' 'Uh-uh: bir-*dddd*.' Before long, the entire juvenile Forest was chanting, 'Saybird-saybirdsaybird,' peer-pressuring Bambi Pavok into saying the difficult word. Eventually, Bambi Pavok did say 'bird' – several times, actually – to great hilarity: 'He speaks! He speaks! Did you hear it? He speaks!' Another time, Bambi Pavok attributed the name 'flower' to, not a flower, but a little skunk by mistake. Hearing this, Fumper fell over with laughter, holding his sides like no one does, ever, outside a cartoon. He was in stitches, hah hah hah hah, over Bambi Pavok calling a skunk a flower. He ended up throwing himself on the floor, rolling onto his stomach, and kicking his legs hysterically, almost indecently. It was so funny and sexy to Fumper, to laugh at Bambi Pavok's expense.

Not altogether surprisingly, Bambi Pavok started toying with the idea of running away. Initially, he suppressed it. Where was he going to run to, anyway? He had nowhere to go. Besides, he'd been told not to run. He'd been told expressly not to mobilise in that fashion, whatever else he was planning on doing, don't run, do stay put, False Widower had said. False Widower of the Forest didn't want his child to go very far. He'd become reliant on his personalised stress ball.

But the nightmares continued and, depending on

which way the wind blew, so did the cooking smell. Eventually, Bambi Pavok remembered his mother's famous last words, which, technically, *literally* even, had been an instruction to run: Faster! Faster, Bambi Pavok! Don't look back! Keep running!

So he did it, he ran. Forest smelling of flowers and frikadellen, Bambi Pavok ran through the woodland, disturbing wilted leaves on the floor. He was done with trepidation, and emboldened by his dead mother's legacy and stand-out survival tip. 'Don't run, Mincemeat Pavok!' Fumper called, barely keeping up with his 'friend'. 'You're not allowed! I'll tell the False Widower!'

While on the subject——. The one thing my own mother did before checking out was, she told me to run. Gave me permission. So I, Corey Fah, ran, far as I could. Left my native Forest and immigrated to the capital, where before long I'd meet Drew and my so-called destiny——.

Červí díra wouldn't have looked like much. Inside a clearing, next to a ditch, Bambi Pavok would've happened across an average wormhole, no more than a metre diameter, burrowing straight down into the Forest's reddish-brown earth in '42, re-emerging, who cared where or when – in this instance, Koszmar Circus, present day, the night I, Corey Fah, was announced the winner of the Award for the Fictionalisation of Social

Evils 2024. Most of us would've given červí díra a very wide berth. Not Bambi Pavok. He saw a way out. He walked up to it, looked down, fancied it and dived in, deliberately. No regard for whose life he'd end up affecting, nor whose priorities he'd interfere with, on the Koszmar Circus side of affairs.

What if I hadn't taken him back with me to Sociální Estate, which I had done against my better judgement. What if I'd left him alone in the international capital, which to him was pretty much the Wild West. What might have happened to him? He hadn't given any of it a second thought.

I shared my concerns about Bambi Pavok with Drew. They weren't impressed. They said, 'Have you lost it, Corey,' and, 'Listen to yourself. It's like you're talking about your younger self, not Bambi Pavok at all.'

'Get out of here,' I replied, and, 'Wtf, Drew.'

Drew said it again, 'Is mad, hating on Bambi Pavok. Is like hating on the undomesticated part of you.'

'Shut up,' I said. Honestly. Drew hadn't a clue what they were talking about. Part of the problem was, I didn't hate Bambi Pavok at all. Whatever I said about him, whatever I kept telling myself on repeat, I loved him a little more every day.

4

Let's get twitterpated.

Drew went Koszmar Circus in the small hours. They opened the cast-iron gate, then let it click shut behind them. Noticing blackthorn, hawthorn and chrysanthemums to either side, they climbed the two sets of stairs leading up the mount. Strange feel to the place. Uncanny. For psychic protection, they pulled their bomber jacket tighter around their shoulders. Once at the top, Drew paused and got their bearings. Circa ten metres ahead of them, under the bandstand, its pyramid-shaped roof, the trophy hovered in situ. It radiated its under- yet overstated perversion of beige.

Drew was personally invested in me having the trophy. They had agreed to do this, not just for me, but for both of us. I'd been high-maintenance lately, but then, wasn't I always. Not easy to live with, Drew would say. I prioritised writing over everything including Drew, and up until recently to scant financial or reputational reward. Drew would come back from a twelve-hour shift in oncology, telling patients they'd been diagnosed with acute lymphoblastic leukaemia, multiple myeloma, adenocarcinoma of the pancreas, in

Slovakian, Polish, or Czech, invasive or non-invasive, HER2-positive, triple-negative, local, regional or distant recurrence, survival rates after five years, after ten, likely the doctors wouldn't commit. No, your hair will not grow back in the way you'd expect. Here's the emergency number you should call. Here's how to join your online support group. Whereas I, I would've sat on the sofa all day, laptop on lap, writing my Substack or my novel, forgetting to put on the lights when it got dark. Point being, Drew carried a lot. They hoped that this prize, this opportunity, if taken advantage of, could be a turning point neither of us had seen coming. If we played this correctly, chances were, I'd be able to start pulling my weight in the future. Start contributing. 'But first, let's get you your trophy,' they'd said. Couldn't be that hard. Or could it.

Drew made their way to the bandstand. Pebbles crunched under their steps, disrupting the silence. Twigs cracked. The trophy jittered, got testy, but for now it stayed put. Could go either way still. Circa a metre or two from their target, Drew stopped. Carefully, carefully, they took off their jacket. Holding it by the shoulders, unfolded, they got in position. They were about to parachute their bomber in the relevant direction when——.

What was that. High-velocity thumping, sounding disproportionately loud. Drew looked around. Movement in the dog rose over there. Again, more insistent. Thump-thump-thump-thump! What *was* it—.

Apprehension rather than curiosity led Drew to stop what they were doing and go have a look. They threw their jacket over their shoulder and made for the shrubbery.

Fumper, a one-toothed rabbit with a white chest, flushed cheeks, and a set of behavioural problems, was in convulsions amid the dog rose. His left foot was pounding the earth. He wasn't alone: another bunny was there, too, seducing him. Drew watched as she started singing, Lah! Lalalah! She went in for a kiss, to the effect that Fumper went all light-headed and swoony-eyed. He brain-bypassed, and went into explicit, and truth be told *disturbing*, fitting: thump-thump-thump-thump! His eyes rolled to the back of his head, was he alright.

The grotesquerie unfurled further. On the level below, a young blue-eyed skunk named Flower succumbed to the allure of another, bluer-eyed skunk, batting her lashes. She kissed him beneath the hydrangeas, triggering what looked like an allergic reaction in her partner. You know when you can't look, but you also can't look away? Drew had no choice but to watch as histamine pink set in around Flower's lips. The blushing proceeded to travel up the skunk's face and forehead, where it lingered for a moment, before progressing down his back, all the way to the tip of his stripy tail. Flower's entire body stiffened, and then he rolled over dead, for all Drew knew. Unexpectedly, he came to, some seconds later. He looked around, noticed Drew watching him, and giggled embarrassedly.

Two blue tits in the plane trees! Bir! Bir! Getting twitterpated.

Now, Drew wasn't a wallflower when it came to sex. Was me who was a bit take-it-or-leave-it in this respect. But this, intense twitterpation? Involving a one-toothed rabbit, who, by the way, looked vaguely familiar? Say nothing of Flower beneath the hydrangeas, enjoying some sexy time. Had Drew beat. Reminded them of these sexualised cartoons they target young children with on the internet, *fuck*. Reminded them also of the fact that people thought nothing of exposing their babies to highly heterosexualised content – like *Bambi* – while supporting legislation against the 'promotion' of homosexuality to minors in all its variable historical guises. For all of these reasons and more, Drew Szumski felt properly spooked.

Prying themselves away from Fumper, Flower and their forgettably named female companions, Drew thought, might as well see where they're all pouring out of. Same hole as Bambi Pavok had a few days ago? Might as well get to the bottom of what's going on at Koszmar Circus, and who knows, encounter a real-life červí díra while they were at it. Rather than make their way back to the bandstand and return to their task, Drew pushed further into the thicket. Don't step on anything. Nothing land on me, please. They lifted the lower branches of rhododendrons with their foot. Wound past spiky-leaved puyas. Scraped their cheek on the frond of a tree fern, while avoiding bottom creepers and stinging nettles wherever possible. Finally, they saw it. There. Under the hawthorn, next to the elder bushes. Beside the pampas grass, quite hidden away. Shit – červí díra. Shit shit shit. Could it be true? Didn't look like much, Drew had to admit. Clean-cut hole in earthy ground, circa a metre diameter, going down steep. No light at the end of it, as far as they could tell. Using the torch app on their phone, Drew could confirm that nothing was pouring out of the suspected červí díra at this moment in time. Nothing was going in, either. They didn't dare drop anything into it, a test object, perhaps. They didn't know what to do full-stop.

Ongoing thumping ricocheted off the apartment blocks surrounding the mount, reminding Drew that this mightn't be the best place to linger. High time to get going. High time to get back to the job at hand. One, two, three lights on now on the estate. The sun was starting to come up when Drew made their way out of the thicket and back to the bandstand.

To Drew's relief, the trophy hadn't moved. It remained a sitting duck. Drew recomposed themselves. Limbered up. Did some breathing exercises. Then they slid their jacket off their shoulder, unfolded it and took aim. Finally, finally, they dispatched it as throw net. It glided as it was meant to glide, glided still, then descended on target. Got you! No resistance as Drew stepped forward, claiming the trophy, all parcelled off. They'd caught it like a wild animal.

'YES! YES!' Flower went in the distance, apropos of what, Drew would rather not know.

This should've been it. The end. Some complications, delays and trepidations, but nothing, really, that Drew hadn't been able to handle. Bonus of a real-life červí díra in direct view. Only it wasn't, the end. About to leave Koszmar Circus with the trophy, Drew felt something heavy, also light, on their shoe. They were surprised to find Fumper the bunny getting close-up and personal with their left Asics Tiger. There he was, forming brand-new attachments. Cute, arguably, but also cursed. Drew lifted their foot including Fumper, and shook it, going, 'Get off me,' and, 'Off with you!' No avail. The rabbit sat tight. Wrapped its front paws round Drew's ankle like an electronic curfew tag. Hooked its incisor into their shoelace. 'Seriously? Ok. Fine. If that's what you want—.' Drew decided to get on their way regardless of their unwanted passenger.

Fumper riding their Asics Tiger, they proceeded to hobble down two sets of stairs.

It wasn't until the iron gate had closed behind Drew that the trophy began to play up. So far remarkably passive, forgiving, even, at this late stage in the proceedings it went off. Realising that Fumper was going wherever it went, perhaps, it started to struggle in Drew's arms. It resisted their hold and made like a trapped thing. Suffice to say, Drew fought. They held on so tight that at one point their feet left the ground. But the trophy wriggled like mad, and, eventually, Drew had to let go. It took off, heading to, wherever, the mythical depot in the sky hoarding the Earth's prestige and cultural capital, Drew didn't know. À bientôt, see you never, and who, really, would blame it. Last thing Drew knew, their bomber jacket fell down from high, landing on the peak of the bandstand's roof, where it hung like a sad little Szumski flag.

Somewhere along their way home, Drew managed to shake Fumper off their trainer. But whether they liked it or not, they were being followed by a small jumping shadow, all the way back to Sociální Estate.

The following afternoon, Drew and I sat on the sofa, decompressing after the previous night's exploits. Fumper sat on the floor, up on his hind legs, licking a single frozen raspberry on the coffee table in front of him. Drew had placed it there. Putting aside their initial objections, they were warming to Fumper already. They were taking pity on him. Typical. As I said, they had love for anything vulnerable, at times to their detriment. In the corner, the television was on mute.

Looking at Fumper, innocent baby. Just having an ice lolly over there, not even a real one. Wasn't fooling me. Personally, I had reservations about him. Bambi Pavok, for one, had been hiding under a duvet since he'd arrived. I felt like doing the same.

Drew told me what had happened at Koszmar Circus, headline being, no trophy. They were sorry.

'Sorry won't get me my trophy,' I said. Fair to say, I responded less forgivingly to Drew's misadventure than they had to any of mine over the years.

This wasn't the outcome Drew'd wanted, either. But they'd said their piece. Nothing else to it. 'Terrible scenes, Corey. Believe. Sorry.'

To be honest, I couldn't get my head round – what Drew say? – twitterpation. Not a colloquialism I was familiar with. Sex was a foreign country to me as it was. Meme going, if ur sex organs were named after the last tv show u watched, what would it be? Not *Gets to the Bottom of It*, incidentally. *Curb Your Enthusiasm*, I'm not even joking. I say it again, Drew was the sexy one out of the two of us.

Frantic licking over at the coffee table. Fumper's

raspberry was melting. Already it sat in a puddle. The shamelessness on display bothered me, especially considering that Bambi Pavok had been rejecting his food since he'd got here. Regardless of Drew's and my efforts to entice him to eat, he'd had nothing. Frozen raspberries, I'd bought them for him. Not interested. Going in Fumper instead.

'Looked really basic, Corey,' Drew said regarding Koszmar Circus červí díra, changing the subject. They picked up the remote and turned up the volume on the tv. Was it that time already? It was — *St Orton Gets to the Bottom of It* came on, with a difference.

The theme tune had been given the genre treatment, horror on the occasion. Barely reminiscent of the original, a Bontempi organ was playing a sequence of diminished chords over sporadic kettle drumming. Dah-deedle-dum BOOM BOOM BOOM. Also, the travelling-through-červí-díra animated title sequence had been recolourised in dark red. It culminated in the regular pinkout with maroon lettering, but the typeface had been changed from, what, regular Blackbaud Sans to Blood Alphabet SVG, with distinct drip effect. What was going on.

'Wow,' I said, 'that's a first.' Running joke was, the show was always the same. Sean didn't see why he should adapt a winning format to suit anyone. He never even did a Christmas special.

Today, there would be no guest, Sean announced. He sat on his chair facing the camera, legs apart, zigzag-patterned boxing shorts gleaming, forearms resting on armrests. He was sweating. Breathing more than usual. In this special episode, he had decided to address his viewers directly. The one in which Sean St Orton doesn't gets to the bottom of it, but to the point.

Eyes on the tv, Drew was stroking a bald patch between Fumper's ears, as I well noticed. Tsk. Way they fell for the troubled ones—.

This was an appeal to viewers, Sean said, to come forward if they had reliable information about actual červí díra activity, and otherwise to practise restraint, stay down whatever hole they considered crawling out of. Had the audience ever wondered why, after four years of trying, Sean had not, in fact, got to the bottom of anything? Why his working theory had barely evolved? His guests had been worthless, that's why. It wasn't like Sean wasn't aware he'd made a career out of having his hopes dashed routinely. Part of what kept viewers watching was the hurt in his expressive working-class face, no feelings were hidden in it. But Friday's show – with Malachi Hölderlin – had been the final straw. He was no longer prepared to feel the feelings of a nation so we didn't have to. Going forward, he wouldn't be giving fantasists and attention-seekers the benefit of the doubt, not like he had been. He wouldn't have his generosity exploited anymore. He'd been *that* close to walking out this morning, but with his fans in mind, and his wage packet, he'd decided to go on-air, today and every weekday thereafter at the regular time. He wouldn't interview guests, though. Oh no. Until such a time that a genuine červí díra would be proposed to him, by a serious guest, via his production team, he refused to fulfil his regular duties as title star and presenter of the TBC's flagship afternoon programme *St Orton Gets to the Bottom of It*.

Captivated by the developments on tv, Drew stopped moving their hand between Fumper's ears momentarily.

For the remainder of today's broadcast, Sean continued, he would play the Bontempi organ over a recording of kettle drums for twenty-five minutes. He would like viewers to take this as an invitation to reflect, look inwards, and ask themselves why they were watching: to see him get to the bottom of it, or to see him get hurt.

Bontempi going bink-a-bink bink.

Fumper going thump-thump-thump-thump.

'Corey,' Drew said.

'What.'

'Would you ever go on the show?'

No. Nononono. I knew it'd been a dream of Drew's to meet Sean St Orton in real life, but I couldn't say the same for myself. 'Not really, Drew. No. Sorry.'

'But Corey, we're sitting on key information.' Didn't I want to hear what Sean had to say about Koszmar Circus červí díra? Didn't I want to get to the bottom of it? Bambi Pavok, Fumper, where did they come from and what'd it all mean? Wasn't I curious? Besides, Drew thought we deserved some fun. Life hadn't been easy lately, and they could do with some light release. Fun, Corey. People had fun. It wasn't that deep.

Raspberry juice dripping onto the floor, ushering the blood effect of the *Gets to* special typeface into our living room.

'Why don't *you* go on, Drew. You saw červí díra. You live with the consequences.'

'Won't have the same weight if I do it, as opposed to Corey Fah, award-winning novelist. C'mon, Corey, do this for me.'

Thump-thump-thump-thump! Again, more urgently – THUMP!

I realised Drew had a wingman. Was as if Fumper was encouraging, challenging, even, Drew to make demands for themselves. Get their own needs met for a change. That's where this was coming from – *don't think I don't see you*, I sent evil thoughts to Fumper the agitator.

Call coming through on my phone.

'Probably Social Evils,' I said.

'Take it,' Drew said, and when I didn't, they said it again, '*Take* it.'

'Hello?' I was looking at Drew.

How did it go. You get the trophy? the prize coordinator wanted to know.

'I didn't, I'm sorry to say.'

You didn't? It didn't reteleport?

'Oh it did. It got away again.'

Silence.

We won't be able to release the funds without the trophy, the prize coordinator said, as if I didn't know. Worse, the annual Social Evils winner event planned for this coming weekend – a reading followed by an audience q&a in the capital's Festival Hall – would have to be put on ice. Until the trophy was recovered, we'd remain in Iceland, Alaska, the freezer compartment, because, how would people differentiate me from the next best, she didn't know, Instagram poet. At this point in the prize cycle, previous winners'd had a couple of profiles in the *Observer*, the *New Times Rwanda*, *El Universal* and tv appearances. They'd be finalising arrangements for an international book tour and a series of lucrative talks at overseas universities. They might have had a TBC radio play commissioned. Me? I'd had initial reports, then nothing. My media presence had fallen off a cliff, as far as the prize coordinator was concerned. Had I put myself out there, at all? Had I made myself available? Prize coordinator didn't think so. Even she hadn't been able to get through to me. She'd emailed, she'd called—.

'I've had a lot going on lately,' I said.

Like what. Most people from my background would kill for the platform. Case of self-sabotage here. Why they (plural pronoun, denoting the international, multiracial working classes) keep doing this to themselves, was incomprehensible to her. Was like, they were throwing the widening participation agenda back into their faces.

Meanwhile, on tv, Sean segued into a live rendition of the *St Orton Gets to the Bottom of It* theme tune. Mini organ on lap, he bent forward as he played. Cheap plastic keys clacking as they were pressed.

'So what we do now,' I said, pragmatically. 'Reteleport again?'

No. Not that easy. Teleportation was not without risks. Also, in what world would the outcome of yet another reteleportation be different. They'd tried twice already.

What risks. 'What if I picked up the trophy, anywhere. Is there a depot? I guess what I'm asking is, where are the trophies kept *before* teleportation?'

Depot? The prize coordinator had never heard anything like it. No. No depot.

Overhearing the conversation, Drew started to look irritated with me. Did I know anything? What sort of novelist was I? Get it together, they mouthed. Corey, please.

Prize coordinator said we were running out of options. We'd arrived at a point where she'd have to involve the literary director of the prize. Consult the prize committee. She'd be in touch. If I could pick up my phone. Respond to my emails.

Call ended without us having resolved anything. Contemplating Drew, Fumper, the raspberry mess down the latter's entire front and the living room floor, I couldn't help thinking it looked like a bloodbath in here. Dah-deedle-dum – uh-oh.

5

Drew is a top, always has been, but they gets to the bottom of it.

The *St Orton Gets to the Bottom of It* studio was situated, not in the TBC Broadcasting House in Central, but not far off in terms of distance at least. In terms of status, it was a million miles south. This was the Friday the week after next, just over three weeks since I'd won the award. Drew, myself and Bambi Pavok found ourselves on a backstreet in the Gheto Attentat part of town, outside what seemed like an evacuated office block. Several windows on the upper floors were broken or boarded up. Desolate feel to the place, not what I'd expected. As per the instructions I'd received, we descended a short external staircase leading to the studio which was located on the lower-ground floor. The front door was closed, scratched black paint, stickers on it. Drew rang the intercom. We were promptly buzzed through. No one received us inside, so we made our way down a black-walled corridor, past a few dressing rooms on the left, leading directly to the live television studio.

I'd ended up agreeing to going on *Gets to*, of course. Drew might have failed to collect at Koszmar Circus, they might have brought Fumper into our home, but taking the longer view, I owed them. Picture us earlier in the flat, getting ready. I'd slicked back my hair for the occasion. Drew had done nothing to theirs. As per usual, they'd outdone me looks-wise with no effort at all. Still, wearing my beige tracksuit bottoms and the light pink sleeveless jumper with the white shirt underneath, I'd felt positive about what I'd realised would be my first public appearance since winning the prize. Who needed a q&a at Festival Hall, I didn't. I'd talked myself into it.

Bambi Pavok would come.

'Really?' Drew'd said, picking up their capacious backpack. 'You're taking him?'

'I am,' I'd replied. I wasn't going to explain myself either. If whatshername, Malachi Hölderlin – the gothy youth without mates or ambitions, and, until now, the last guest on *St Orton Gets to the Bottom of It* – had thought nothing of bringing her rabbit, I'd bring Bambi Pavok. 'You're not taking Fumper, though, are you,' I'd asked. Leading question.

Drew's backpack had betrayed them. It'd been moving the entire time. Hadn't been staying still for a minute. Thing thumping away in there, impossible not to notice.

Back in the studio, Drew and I were having our respective feelings. The former was awestruck just being in the space, so familiar from tv. In reality, the

Gets to studio was a windowless room the size of an 'intimate' nightclub with a green screen mounted against the far wall. The iconic grey leather swivel chairs were positioned in front of it, at present unoccupied. Three cameras on tripods were facing the scene, and so was the three-tier grandstand with flip-up seats, currently up. Again, not what I'd imagined. Place looked smaller than on tv. Unassuming.

Meanwhile, Bambi Pavok gave in to an impulse to cut loose. He bolted towards the grandstand. He didn't go up, explore the seating area, perhaps, but disappeared underneath.

'You today's guest? Corey Fah, plus one?' The first person to acknowledge our presence introduced herself as Sean's PA. She said she would take us to a pre-meet with the host in his dressing room. If we could follow her. No sign of Bambi Pavok, so I left him behind. Didn't think anything of it. We'd be back shortly.

After a walk along the corridor, the PA knocked on one of the doors coming off it, and opened it without waiting for a response.

Inside, Sean sat on a sofa, trainers on the coffee table in front of him. He was wearing a boxing robe, open, and his regular shorts. He looked up but didn't get up as we walked in. 'Chairs,' he said. They were somewhere. Ah!

Back there——. He indicated a stack of chairs in the corner of his remarkably untidy dressing room.

Drew was elated to see Sean. Actually overcome, flushed in the face. Aw. This was worth it, I thought, first time since we'd got here. More than anyone, myself included, Drew deserved a bit of happiness. They manoeuvred past a bucket of fake gore by the side of the sofa, a themed prop that'd had more than its fair share of use over the course of the past thirteen days of Sean's action short of strike. They took down two of the chairs, and set them up for us near the door. The PA had left without anyone noticing.

'Well, well,' Sean said, looking me up and down. 'Who we got here. Corey Fah, winner of this year's Award for the Fictionalisation of Social Evils.'

I didn't know what to say. Self-same?

Only reason Sean had agreed to have a guest on already, and disrupt the withdrawal of his labour which he'd been prepared to extend indefinitely, was because it was me, Corey Fah. He had been surprised when his producer told him I wanted to come on the show.

'This is Drew,' I said, putting my hand on their back as if pushing them forward in their chair.

Sean gave Drew the once-over and approved, who wouldn't, but subsequently returned his focus to me. Did I know, he'd been a playwright in his former life.

'So you say. Shit-hot.'

He'd won the exact same prize, Social Evils, in 1967.

'You did?'

He did. No one believed him though. He'd won, not as Sean St Orton, which was a pseudonym, but under his real name. Did I?

Did I what.

Believe him.

How about some small talk, I thought. How about offering us some of the finger sandwiches on the dressing table over there, preferably without cucumber.

'*I* believe you,' Drew said, keenly.

He didn't speak about his prize anymore, Sean continued, nor his former career as a writer. Couldn't, in fact. His family had taken out an injunction, preventing him from using or publicly mentioning his own name. They'd thought him a fraud. When he'd first arrived in this timeline in 2014, sticking point had been that, unlike the playwright, who'd been thought dead since '67, killed in the attack he'd escaped, Sean had been alive. Also, Sean had been way too young to be who he'd claimed to be – thirty-four years of age, when the playwright would've been eighty-one, YOB being 1933. Surviving sisters and brothers-in-law had never got onto the červí díra bandwagon, they'd plain refused to entertain the possibility of time travel. As a result, they'd lacked access to the conceptual framework that would've allowed them to make sense of everything, including the age discrepancy.

Imagine being ousted from your own life, Sean said, including the achievements of your past. He'd spent years trying to prove his identity. He'd pleaded with his family, look, it's me! Use your eyes! He'd taken DNA tests. He'd released personal details only the playwright could know. No avail. Eventually, he'd decided to stop wasting his life trying to convince people who didn't want to know. He'd had to accept that, in '14, he was nobody. A man without history, and certainly not the recipient of a prestigious literary award. In other words, he'd had to start over. Observing the injunction, he'd changed his name to Sean St Orton and dedicated himself to gets to the bottom of it, both the technicalities of what had happened to him, and the show.

'The long-term plan is to return to my previous life. Once I'll have worked out how, and I will, work out how, I'll get myself back to '67. Won't be blindsided, either. See these boxing gloves, on the commode? For self-defence. Domestic situation, if you recall. If I end up back there, I'll be prepared. I've been training. Given the chance, I'll take anyone out.' Sean whacked his right fist into the palm of his left hand for emphasis, sitting forward.

Drew and I leant back in our respective chairs.

'What about the public,' I asked. 'How come no one recognised you in '14 or since, if you were so well known in the sixties?' Just saying. It seemed incongruous. Even my photo had been in the papers a few weeks ago on account of the prize. His would've been.

Ah! He had lil theory, Sean was smart. Our generation and the generation before, if we had heard of him, did indeed have an idea of what he, the playwright, had looked like in '67 – but it wasn't *this*, Sean indicating his entire body. Instead, the contemporary public imagined him as the actor who'd played him in a famous biopic from 1987, Marek Oldman. In other words, he, sixties playwright, had been replaced by Marek Oldman in the collective imagination. Despite his visibility as a daytime presenter, it was perfectly possible that no one should recognise him, certainly no one with social power. The odd old-age pensioner might, but who listened to those in an ageist society. Besides, he'd changed, physically that is, even since first he'd entered this timeline. He'd never reached his mid-forties in the past, so the chances of anyone recognising him were getting slimmer by the day.

Marek Oldman, huh? How about I played a few notes on the Bontempi organ leaning against the wall over there, violin preset, perhaps, underline the melodrama—. Drew pushed their elbow into my side, meaning behave. They wanted me to say something supportive. Express solidarity, from one prizewinner to another. But I didn't want to. I found Sean snide in person and arrogant. I didn't like him sitting there with his legs apart, winning my prize and winking at Drew. Way he had winked at Drew a couple of times while he'd been talking. Who even does that.

Drew said they'd heard of the playwright whose name couldn't be mentioned for legal reasons. They even had a vague idea of what he'd looked like. White guy with dark brown hair and brown eyes, wasn't it. White t-shirts with high roll-up jeans, usually worn with a statement belt – *vaguely* like Sean, but not *like* Sean.

'Oldman,' Sean said, coldly. Marek Oldman. His least favourite actor in the world. Please help yourselves to some finger sandwiches, by the way. Yes, take the clingfilm off. None of them come without cucumber, why would they.

'So, when Wikipedia says the playwright was killed . . .'

Do I look dead to you. Sean had escaped through červí díra that'd opened in his studio flat, like he'd said. He had another lil theory, he wasn't not sharp. In his experience, people were quite content to believe in travel through time and space, but they fundamentally didn't believe that a working-class homo, met with that level of success, could or should be surviving long-term. If you aren't cut out for it, meaning social-ised accordingly, if it's not in your physical make-up or your family history, don't go flying too close to the sun, bird, or it'll cost you. Whether consciously or unconsciously, people preferred him dead. Kept their received world order intact.

First thing Sean had said that got my attention. I'd have asked him to elaborate, but his PA put her head through the door. 'Fifteen minutes before we go live,' she said. 'Let's get you all set.'

The studio was busy now. Camera operators were in situ, testing their equipment and talking to each other. Strips of gaffer tape in mouth, a technician made last-minute adjustments to the overhead microphones. Various spotlights came on and went off again. Simultan-eously, an audience coordinator was ushering thirty or so members of the public towards their seats, not quite a full house: the regular motley crew of enthusiasts, tour-ists, sceptics and a sprinkling of enemies – Sean's appeal bridged demographics.

Drew had taken their seat in the front row, bul-ging backpack under their chair. They gave me the thumbs-up.

I was sitting up front on one of the swivel chairs, way more worn than was appreciable on tv. A sound technician was fitting a lapel mic to the neckband of my jumper. In the chair next to me sat the famous host. Unlike me, he wore a headset with an earpiece, which he appeared to be cursing right now. A control monitor had been positioned in front of us, currently running a test pattern. I'd been informed that, once we went live, it would display the show as it was broadcast. If in doubt, I should look at the monitor – I'd see what viewers at home would see. I took a sip of water out of one of the glasses that had been placed on the floor by our chairs. Looking out onto the studio audience, I gave Drew the thumbs-up back.

Sean hadn't asked me anything about the červí díra I'd come on to discuss, a lack of preparation which I assumed was part of his method. Sean'd find out what was what at the same time as his viewers, allowing him to deliver the seemingly unmediated live experience we'd come to expect and look forward to. Had I known the extent to which we were all unprepared for what was about to happen, I'd have got up and walked out.

'Stand by,' the director said. 'We're live in fifteen seconds—.' The *Gets to* theme tune came on, the familiarity of which, I believe, prompted Bambi Pavok to crawl out of his hidey-hole under the grandstand. No one saw him but me. With the audience coordinator's back towards him, Bambi Pavok stood in the access corridor having a good look around.

There. We made eye contact, which Bambi Pavok

took as an invitation to come hurtling towards me. He jumped onto my lap, hiding his face in my crotch. MO was dissociation still, so I froze. Already, the title sequence was moving into its latter half. In a matter of seconds, I'd be broadcasting Bambi Pavok to the world and I wasn't ready for it. I might never be.

Sean signalled to get rid. Now.

I pushed, I pulled. I cursed his dead mother, to no avail – Bambi Pavok refused to get up.

Ok, keep him on your lap, then. Calm. Keep him calm. What even is it. Eight legs, four sets of eyes, Sean had never seen anything like it. He červí-díra-related?

I looked at Sean. What do *you* think.

The title sequence ended in classic dirty pink, with maroon title. Held the image for a second, and we were live. Wide shot of Sean and myself – with Bambi Pavok – on the control monitor, as well as on tv sets and phone screens worldwide.

'Good afternoon, studio audience and viewers at home. After thirteen days of musical protest, normal service will resume temporarily. I'm sure you'll agree the occasion demands it: please join me in welcoming the recent recipient of the Award for the Fictionalisation of Social Evils, Corey Fah, to the show. That's some credentials, huh, Corey Fah? They are here with—'

'—Bambi Pavok,' I said.

'Bambi Pavok,' Sean repeated. Moving on swiftly, 'So what brings you here, Corey. What can you tell me about červí díry that I haven't already heard?' There was that mocking tone again. Guy really got jaded, not a good look. And yet, the studio audience was lapping it up, including Drew on their front-row seat.

Camera was panning towards me and, inevitably, Bambi Pavok. Sensing eyes on him, the latter came alive. He lifted his head and turned to the camera. Spotting himself on the control monitor, he – finally, belatedly, and with previously unimaginable urgency – leapt off my lap. Not that he moved out of shot, no. He stood as if electrified, ears pricked up, staring directly into the camera, then back to the monitor, the camera, the monitor, the camera, and into hundreds of thousands of living rooms internationally. Huh! He noticed the červí díra animation on the monitor, seemingly behind him. He turned round and walked right up to the green screen to investigate – closer, pushing his face into it. No červí díra, just a rancid-tasting green screen, a deposit of the tears, sweat and saliva of thousands of studio guests, audience members and tv crew. Bleurgh. Done here, Bambi Pavok proceeded to walk to the left, to the right, then up to the front again. Ultimately, he positioned himself centre-stage, in front of Sean and myself, peering out into the audience unnervingly.

Crowd reaction varied from, wow, who he, where

did he come from, which wormhole did he crawl out of? To, look at that, making a show of himself. Has to be centre of attention, distracting from Sean St Orton, červí díra specialist, and Corey Fah, award-winning author. Impossible to concentrate on what either of them might have to say, what with that going round. This child-friendly, by the way? PG-rated? TBC afternoon slot?

If the monitor was anything to go by, the control room had decided to run with it. Camera work focused on Bambi Pavok, reducing Sean and myself to passive observers. The special-effects people were feeding in background illustrations suggesting a forest: impressionistic swashes of browns, pinks and purples, white firs and pines, all swaying behind us, apparently, in an imaginary breeze.

Funny how, in certain lights, certain environments, Bambi Pavok's eyes appeared red.

White parent with white child got up and walked out, judging the performance unsuitable. They were the exception: everyone else was caught up in the Bambi Pavok show. I alone noticed the subplot unfold. Under Drew's chair, someone inside a backpack was feeling excluded. Was desperate to participate, breathe some studio air. Employing his front tooth, Fumper unzipped Drew's Eastpak from the inside. Rabbit's ear flipped out first. Vehement wriggling, and the head came out. Fumper gauged the situation at ankle level: all clear. Writhing like mad, he proceeded to belly-flop onto the studio floor, wielding his body into the public arena. I, and only I, watched him recover and make his way towards the front, the grey leather swivel chairs, not so much bunny-hopping as spy-crawling, the word was stealth.

Catching a scent, Bambi Pavok tensed. His nostrils flared. Red, did I say, his eyes signalled danger.

Call it a sixth sense, I had a bad feeling. 'Don't,' I said, instinctively. No use.

It happened so quickly. Bambi Pavok lunged forward, pouncing. Really pouncing, was a nightmare. Next thing I or anyone knew, Fumper was pinned to the floor, legs akimbo, Bambi Pavok standing over him.

Audience going whoa, getting up off their seats and craning their necks. Two, three, four people walked out – beat a retreat, more like.

Camera operator went in up close, broadcasting live. Unfazed, Bambi Pavok opened his mouth, and out came an arcane MOUTHPART, shaped like a DRINKING STRAW, an anatomical detail that he'd inherited from his father, that had travelled down the paternal line through generations of False Widowers of the Forest. The secret was out, literally: digestive fluid was dripping from its tip.

At the receiving end, Fumper was wriggling and squirming. With Bambi Pavok employing six legs to restrain him, just two for stabilisation, bunny had no hope of freeing himself. Fumper was stew.

Out of the corner of my eye, I saw the audience coordinator block Drew, keep them from intervening. Consensus among the crew was, this was the mother lode of daytime tv, long may it continue. We are broadcasting live from the Gheto Attentat studio, stay with us for kicks!

Meanwhile, Bambi Pavok proceeded to sluice onto Fumper's abdomen while simultaneously sucking up pre-digested fur and tissue.

On the monitor, I watched the thick drip-down effect making a comeback: the backdrop to the main action was turning red from top to bottom. Discordant Bontempi stabs, pre-recorded, rang through the studio speakers. Sean hadn't known what a horror show was until Bambi Pavok'd come along, I thought, gleefully. As it was, the host looked pale and oddly irrelevant. Things were slipping away from him and he knew it.

All of this happened within, what, ten, fifteen seconds. Apart from Drew, no one had even attempted to stop the attack. By the time I myself leapt up and pulled Bambi Pavok off his victim, there was little left of the latter.

Ten minutes into the show, the end sequence started up on the monitor. The control room, who'd been instrumental in pushing the theme, must've received a top-down order to go off-air, yet again prematurely. *St Orton Gets to the Bottom of It* was fast becoming a liability for the TBC, plain to see.

In the studio, the houselights went up. 'Everybody, please remember to take your belongings,' the audience coordinator instructed, evacuating the place. 'That's it, nice and easy. This isn't a drill. All the best from the entire *Gets to* team, see you again, thank you, thank you.' One person protested they hadn't heard from the acclaimed author. Teenagers asked about Bambi Pavok, was he ok? Sean! Seany! Noticeably, no one cared about Fumper the rabbit. What was left of him lay on the floor in plain sight, disregarded by everyone.

Drew. Where was Drew. They'd be devastated. Ah! I spotted them all the way at the back by the green screen, with Sean St Orton, incidentally. As predicted, they looked upset. Not *that* upset, if I'm honest. Sean seemed to be comforting Drew. The two of them were talking and sticking their heads together. Laughing. Putting their hands on each other's arms. Wtf—.

As for me? During my first-ever appearance on live tv, I'd landed no more than two words. I'd as good as forgotten my name, never mind the title of my award-winning book. I'd failed to get to the bottom of anything, and I hadn't had fun, particularly. As it was, I was kneeling in front of the world-famous swivel chairs, wiping leftovers off Bambi Pavok's blessed face with a tissue. 'There, there, Bambi Pavok,' I said. 'There, there.'

6

Where's Sean.

On the following Monday, *St Orton Gets to the Bottom of It* wasn't on. Unforeseen circumstances et cetera, we'll broadcast instead, a rerun of *Countryfile*. A nineties wild-life programme set in Chernobyl. Next day, it still wasn't back on. On Wednesday, *Gets to* was returning, or so it seemed. The theme tune started up at three pm prompt. I could see the relief in Drew, their shoulders relaxing. But who was that. The show was hosted, not by St Orton, but by an actress known for her role in the Ghanaian remake of a US tv series about two federal agents investigating unexplained phenomena. Said she'd be filling in for the wonderful Sean today, what a trip. Perhaps controversially, she'd be taking a sceptical position in regards to wormholes, no disrespect. Thanks to the TBC for letting her bring her own slant to the classic show, even if temporarily. She wished to reassure viewers expressly that Sean would be back in a couple of days——. Nah. Drew switched off the tv.

'I like her,' I protested. 'Prefer her, even.'

Drew didn't bother replying. What now, they blamed me for Sean's no-show? They'd been blaming me for practically everything these last few days: going on *Gets to*, I'd ruined it. Say nothing about Fumper who may or may not have deserved what he'd had coming. Besides, I'd made no progress securing my trophy. Remember, the trophy? Ten k prize money? Personally, I'd have liked to remind Drew that I'd already faced the music, and accepted the consequences for the *Gets to* debacle, more of that later. Suffice to say, I'm not seeing Bambi Pavok anywhere. Are you, Drew. Are you seeing Bambi Pavok? Didn't think so. Still, I'd kept shtum.

On our way home from the studio, Drew had sat on the bus with Fumper's remains on their lap, inside a plastic bag. They weren't able to look at me, nor Bambi Pavok. 'You shouldn't have brought him,' they said, meaning the latter. *You* shouldn't have brought *him*, I thought, meaning Fumper, now leaking a little through a hole in the bag. 'What did Sean want, at the end?' I asked. 'Hook up in the men's toilet,' Drew replied. 'Eugh,' I said. Drew didn't say eugh back. Didn't seem like the thought of hooking up with Sean in the lavatory was revolting to them. I didn't know what to make of that.

I never found out what Drew did with the plastic bag. Later that night, I got up and looked for it, but they'd hid it good. Finding the bag, its contents, could've saved me a moderate fortune – money I didn't have. Butcher's in the former doctor's surgery on estate?

I went in early the next morning. Bought an entire rabbit, mercifully anonymous. Some chicken legs for good measure, always assuming that Bambi Pavok's behaviour had been motivated by pent-up hunger, rather than the prospect of getting back at a childhood bully on live tv.

On Thursday, Sean's substitute still was presenting the show. At this point, I had to admit that something felt off. Where *was* Sean. Official explanation was not forthcoming. Naturally, speculation went wild in the fandom. Sean was depressed, went the discourse. He'd finally located a červí díra, and gone for good. He or his ghost had been sighted near Graceland, Tennessee, and the outline of his face had appeared in babyccino froth, to a supermarket cashier, in a café on the outskirts of the capital. By the following Monday, the new presenter was gone. *Gets to* fandom pretty territorial, I said. Ungenerous, racist and misogynist. Drew agreed, to be fair. News finally came that same evening. Sean St Orton, host of the popular TBC One show *St Orton Gets to the Bottom of It*, had made the not altogether unexpected decision to take an indefinite break from presenting. To be clear, this was a *decision* he'd *made*, it wasn't like he'd gone AWOL or anything. The programme would be suspended until further notice. The showrunner and production team would take the occasion to do some soul-searching, ask critical questions about the show's format, its viability, whether and how best to take it into the future, and, if appropriate, conduct a search for St Orton's long-term successor.

'Seany moved on. Greener pastures, et cetera,' I said, as if to see if I'd get away with it.

Drew looked at me, are you mad. Greener pastures, is that so. In reality, I was getting worried and Drew knew it. I had every reason to.

I started having nightmares, the sort I hadn't experienced in my adult life. Most nights I relived the following, more or less: I'd notice a meat smell, subtle at first, like at the estate butcher's. I realised I was in what superficially looked like our living room, the regular rubber tree in the corner and all, but what really was a meat processing plant. I knew this because there were clues, such as the stainless steel shelves fitted against the left wall. They were stacked with hundreds of small, white Styrofoam trays, fistful of mincemeat on each, individually wrapped in several layers of clingfilm. Wearing a hairnet, rubber gloves and a plastic apron, I sat on the familiar linoleum floor in front of my designated workstation. It consisted of a pristine, cut-open and splayed-out plastic bag, and a meat cleaver, ready for use. I was expected to process the 'meat', which, as it turned out, was my co-worker next to me: Bambi Pavok, wearing a hairnet and apron identical to my own. Bambi Pavok had received the exact same instructions, namely to hack away, using his hooves if need be, or the claws at the tips of his spidery legs, at the worker to *his* left – Sean St Orton. Signifying seniority in the hierarchy of the meat processing plant, Sean was wearing a classic white butcher's trilby made from wipeable mesh material. He, too, was chopping away at the co-worker on his left, which I gathered was myself.

Every night, the convergence of human resources and meat supply seemed a false economy to me, not to say uncollegial and really fucking painful. I tried in vain to communicate the perceived inefficiency of the set-up we were complicit in to my co-workers. Bambi Pavok didn't listen, and Sean responded by flinging the fillet of meat he'd just carved out of my lower back towards the balcony doors. It stuck to the glass briefly, before sliding down, leaving a smear. Repressing my disgust, I appreciated Sean was trying to tell me something: looking out of the window, I saw that a queue of replacement workers ready to take our place extended out the front door and through the length of estate. Pay must be lucrative at the meat processing plant, I suddenly thought, feeling the privilege of being inside. I always wished I'd wake up at this point, but I usually didn't. The dream went on and on, and then stayed with me throughout the day.

My other nightmare was a waking one. First time

in twenty years since we'd been together, I thought there was a possibility that I might lose Drew. Their frustration with me showed in every way: for starters, they didn't turn up for the three pm tv slot anymore. I suggested we find something else to watch. Had never been about Sean St Orton anyway and always about us. No, Drew wasn't interested. They took on extra shifts at work, and when they were home, they were always online. They'd joined several *Gets to* forums which they thought more reliable than the TBC news in regards to any updates. One day, I found them sitting on the sofa, talking to themselves and stress-eating frozen raspberries straight from the bag. This isn't good, they kept saying, meaning Sean's disappearance. This isn't good, Corey. Drew, I said, and again, *Drew*. Took them a minute to hear me. This is *bad*, they said, scaring me.

All the while my Gmail was pinging with messages from friends and Substack subscribers who'd seen me on tv. Iconic, Corey. Who's the new pet. Also, emails from Social Evils prize coordinator requesting I be in touch ASAP, publicity management. Something had come up. I already knew Social Evils wanted to speak with me, I'd been ignoring their calls. I suspected my appearance on TBC One was not the kind of media attention they wished to attract, or be associated with. Actually, I wondered whether the prize coordinator had heard of Sean St Orton, who after all claimed to have won the prize in '67? Might ask, given the opportunity. Maybe it didn't matter anymore.

What's that, something from the TBC in my inbox. The showrunner of *St Orton Gets to the Bottom of It* thanking me for my recent appearance on the show. It had stayed with him. Matter of fact, I had left an impression on the entire team. He was writing to invite me to interview for the role of St Orton's successor. Producers were keen to switch up the format, and I, it was thought, was the obvious candidate for the job.

I read that again.

Immediate thought was, I needed politely to decline. My involvement with *Gets to* had become too close for comfort as it was. Thanks for your interest, I replied. Regretfully, I can't. I have a lot going on, it never ends, with me. Besides, I'm not a tv presenter, but a writer, in case you haven't noticed. Award-winning.

Same as Sean, came the response. That's what the showrunner'd been led to believe anyway. I'd be ideal. Think on it, Corey. They'd consider something script-based going forward, if I preferred. I could head up the writers' room. Would that tip the balance for me.

He had my attention. Head up the writers' room. Head writer Corey Fah. Head. Writer. I envisaged a TBC staff card on a branded lanyard round my neck, or dangling from my jogger pocket. What do you think, Bambi Pavok. Should I go and present *St Orton*

Gets to the Bottom of It? Write for it, too? Bambi Pavok? Bambi Pav——. Oh. Bambi Pavok wasn't there anymore. I forgot.

Not sure, I replied. I had a trophy to retrieve. Go on international book tour. Appear in the literary press.

Showrunner didn't know what was, the literary press. Sounded thrilling, though. Not. How about I came up to the new production site mid-next week? No obligations, just a tour round the vicinity and a chat.

OK!!! I typed. Send.

What had just happened. What had I done.

'You ok, Corey?' Drew was about to go out the door, working a late shift.

I told them I was considering a spell on tv.

'Really, Corey. Take over from Sean? Meet the *Gets to* showrunner? That's bold. That's *bold*.' Drew sounded and looked even more upset than I'd expected.

This was why: aside from Drew's loyalty to their star, there was something that neither of us was quite saying, or fully admitting to ourselves at this point. Let's just say that, in lieu of Bambi Pavok, there was an elephant in the room. AS OF SATURDAY AFTERNOON A WEEK AND A HALF AGO, BAMBI PAVOK HAD BEEN REPLACED BY A TERRIBLE ELEPHANT IN DREW'S AND MY LIVING ROOM. Truth be told, St Orton's disappearance might not have been unrelated to what we, Corey Fah and

Drew Szumski, had gone and done that Saturday afternoon, the day after Bambi Pavok had incriminated himself, and me, on live television. Chances were, we'd killed Sean St Orton by accident.

They'd moved production out of the derelict but otherwise regular tv studio in Gheto Attentat and into the open air. Prokletý Field was the site of what once had been the capital's largest stadium. Now only ruins remained. Imagine ten-thousand-seater stands with large craters where the floor had fallen in. Circa two-thirds of the pink plastic seats had been taken out of their fittings. Some had been stacked into metres-high pillars along the side of the former pitch, but had long fallen over. They lay there like earthworms unable to repair themselves. The pitch itself was, overgrown is an understatement: tall grasses and wildflowers were vying with ferns and thistles for whatever sunlight touched down here. On the day, hardly any. The wind whipped across the wide-open space, chasing thunderclouds.

'Drew,' I said, 'see this.' Towards the back of the pitch, near the stadium's east curve, a giant scoreboard had been mounted to the top of an exceptionally high scaffold. Rather than a conventional score, it displayed a live countdown – starting at 8,760 hours, the number of hours in one single prize year, as I was about to find out. In 7,757 hours, zero minutes and ten seconds, that is, 8,760 hours minus 1,002 hours, fifty-nine minutes and fifty seconds – the six weeks to the day that had passed since award night had been accounted for – Social Evils would announce next year's winner. My fifteen minutes would have passed. My window of opportunity would have closed. In the short time it took for Drew and I to get our bearings, seconds fell off the countdown of my life, then minutes, and by the time we would leave, hours. As I was watching, a magpie settled on top of the scoreboard.

Other than that, no sign of a young tv production anywhere at Prokletý Field. 'They must be inside,' Drew said, pointing to the players' tunnel. 'Let's go,' I agreed. We went on our way, avoiding puddles and muddy rivulets like milky tea that pervaded the ex-pitch.

Drew'd guessed correctly. The TBC crew had set up a production hub in the former changing rooms. Place was a building site. No windows or furniture, other than the wooden benches that had been stacked up and converted into makeshift desks. Circa fifteen crew members were present, some looking up, nodding, as we walked in. Two technicians with fashion moustaches were craning their necks, checking the space around Drew's and my legs. Disappointed at the Bambi-Pavok-shaped vacancy there, they shrugged and left the room. Ah! Blond white guy with black-plastic-framed glasses and pre-washed jeans left the gaffer he'd been talking to and came over to us. He introduced himself as the showrunner, I forget his name. 'Let me catch you up,' he said, 'see what you think.'

According to the showrunner, they would continue with a quasi-horror theme, not in a Bontempi-organ-and-bloody-gore kind of way, but in a watch-the-protagonist-fuck-it kind of way. Wormholes were out. The crew were so over wormholes. Drew registered that the showrunner rejected the technical term, červí díry, not just disrespecting the original host, but effectively undertaking the work of his erasure. *Gets to* had never been about wormholes anyway, the showrunner continued, but about watching someone, Sean, pursue their dream, albeit misguidedly, and continually, reliably, fuck it, getting fucked, not in a good way and in public. People didn't exactly love watching someone get crushed on repeat, but neither could they look away. So, the remake would retain a watch-through-your-fingers, edge-of-your-seat type sensibility, but they'd replace Sean's let's be honest delusional attempts to understand spatiotemporal irregularities, with me, Corey Fah, trying to capitalise on my win. Thumbs-up, grotesque grin. Also, it'd be a race against time. 'See the scoreboard on the live monitor up there?' A control screen had been mounted in the corner, under the ceiling, like a television set in a generic hospital room. On it, the giant scoreboard was swaying dangerously on account of the weather conditions. Seconds counting down, always. Tick tock. They really weren't hanging around, I thought. Hardly three weeks since St Orton had gone, and his replacement was nearly complete. In a corner, I spotted the notable swivel chairs, under a plastic cover. A Styrofoam cup of builder's tea had been abandoned on one of the armrests, bag still floating inside.

They'd come up with a few working titles, show-runner continued, subject to discussion with me, of course, and final approval by the TBC. What did I think of Corey Fah does social mobility. Corey Fah is given the chance of their life and then fucks it, repeatedly. How about Corey Fah has 7,453 hours remaining to make their win work for them. They have 6,435 hours to get it together. 'Corey Fah fails at success,' Drew came up with, unhelpfully. Try! Try! was another contender, whereas Corey Fah fails to fail better had definitely, irrevocably, been ruled out. At present, the team were thinking about introducing an added incentive. Raise the stakes, if I wished. In the event that I would, in fact, get it together; if at some point during the scheduled run of the show I did end up defying the odds and manage to retrieve the trophy, and/or otherwise take advantage of my win, the TBC would match the ten k prize money from Social Evils. How about that, Corey Fah. If not, I could count on a pro rata presenter's fee of one hundred pounds per episode presented – until such a time that the show's concept ran its natural course, or the ratings crashed, whichever came first.

'Hundred, seems low,' I said.

'Public sector tv,' the showrunner said, as if that explained it.

For a long time, neither of us said anything.

Could I bring on Drew? I asked, eventually. Who? Drew. My partner. As what. In what capacity. I didn't know, but Drew was fundamentally tied up with any chance of myself succeeding. No. Showrunner was not uninterested in Bambi Pavok, though. Your right-hand boy. Where was he, by the way. His absence had been making waves already and not the positive kind. 'Noticed half the staff walked out when you first came in?' the showrunner asked. They'd been there for Bambi Pavok. They'd lingered solely in the hope of Bambi Pavok making an appearance, their interest in me was perfunctory.

'He isn't here,' I replied. Even if I were to decide to come on as a presenter, involving Bambi Pavok would not be an option.

'Why not?'

Drew and I exchanged a look. Neither of us responded.

Ok, now that I'd effectively put a gun to his head, showrunner had to tell me that the entire deal hinged on Bambi Pavok's participation. Matter of fact, his superiors at the TBC had given the remake the go-ahead only under the condition that Bambi Pavok would be involved. Unlike himself, the showrunner's higher-ups didn't see my, Corey Fah's, personal appeal. They thought it a little marginal. But the killer fawn? Had them in stitches. So. How about Bambi Pavok came on every other day? Too much? Once a week?

I looked at Drew for support. They shrugged, what you want me to say.

The wind howled as we exited through the players' tunnel, eerily changing pitch. Blows away hesitations, the showrunner said as we stepped into the elemental surroundings of Prokletý Field stadium. Reveals the bigger picture. Let's talk about how, in detail, we might bring Corey Fah doing social mobility into the stadium and onto television screens every day. Skeletal script, fleshed out by improv? Would that appeal? Personally, showrunner was très open-minded. As far as he was concerned, everything including the overriding concept was provisional. For all he cared, I could read out some of that novel of mine, was that still relevant? He could make anything work in this environment, and with Bambi Pavok on board. Regarding the latter——. The showrunner was happy to let him loose on the ex-pitch, and film him spiking rats, feral dogs, whatever else lived in the undergrowth, with that mouthpart of his. 'Scenes,' he concluded, looking at me as if conspiratorially. Actual scenes.

The showrunner, Drew and I stood in a row, taking in the desolation of Prokletý Field with diverging feelings. The stands were higher, the grass greyer, the scoreboard larger, even, than first I'd realised, and the seconds it continued to drop seemed unnaturally short. It felt like we'd reached a point in the negotiations where my consent to proceed was taken as a given.

7

Bambi Pavok meets a prominent playwright in '67.

Drew Szumski kicked open the now-familiar gate to Koszmar Circus, letting me know they'd rather be any-where else. Instead of climbing the stairs leading up to the bandstand, Drew veered straight left and into the ground-level thicket. 'Want me to show you červí díra, Corey? I'll show you červí díra,' they shouted, pushing ugly ferns to the side, weaving through bottom creepers. They didn't want to try relocate červí díra they'd found weeks ago. They didn't want to help implement what they considered my mean-spirited plan.

This is going back to the Saturday circa three weeks ago: the day *after* I'd gone on *St Orton Gets to the Bottom of It*, and *before* the show would drop off the tv schedule the following Monday. We came to Koszmar Circus to deport Bambi Pavok. Send him back to where he'd come from, the Forest, '42. What Drew referred to as our Go Home campaign, a barely disguised dig at me. Despite everything, Fumper, Drew was in favour of letting Bambi Pavok stay. Getting rid, they said, was not a solution. 'He's yours,' they said, or, 'He's you,' I don't know, I did not pay attention. They said we'd be better off housetraining him. Impose a programme of soft domestication which would take some dedication on my part. Also, they didn't think it was safe for Bambi Pavok to go back. False Widower? Extensive deer cull? Frikadellen industrial complex of the Forest? Empty threats, most likely, I said, regarding the latter. False Widower was liar king fucking wasteman, everyone knew. In my opinion, Bambi Pavok was good to go. After what he'd done, to Fumper, my relationship with Drew and my reputation, I didn't see how I could let him stay. He'd been really well fed this morning, too. Rabbit and chicken legs from estate butcher's in him. Know what meat costs? As I said, the butcher's was the only one on estate thriving.

Top boy himself? Hadn't a clue what was going on. After three, four weeks of living with Drew and myself, his English was still so shit. He'd never tried very hard. Didn't want to fit in. Way he was trampling the pampas grass over there. Digging up the hydrangeas.

'It's not here,' Drew declared, after what felt to me too short a period of time.

'Well, let's look round the upper tier?'

No reply, but Drew changed direction and made for the stairs. They went up, turned into the walkway circumventing tier one, then pushed into the higher-up shrubbery. 'Don't know what makes you think červí díra will still be here,' Drew said, pushing palm fronds out of their way. None of the available data gave any indication of wormhole stability, or lack thereof. Sean himself was unclear as to whether, once open, červí díry stayed open, or ultimately disappeared. If Drew remembered correctly, Sean was inclined to assume the latter. It would make sense: he'd never managed to recover the červí díra that had landed him, Sean, in 2014. Drew stopped in mid-rant. There it was. Beneath the hawthorn. Among the elder bushes.

'That it?' I said, walking up.

Drew was positive. As far as they were concerned, we were looking down a genuine červí díra, presenting as a bottomless hole in the ground. Drew wouldn't be Drew if they didn't get a little excited at this point. They just wished we were here under different circumstances.

To my eyes, červí díra looked disappointingly basic. 'Bambi Pavok!' I called. 'Over here.' For once, Bambi Pavok came running when called, wide-eyed like some ingénue which I was well aware was a façade. 'Look there,' I said, pointing. 'Pretty wormhole.' Bambi Pavok walked up to its edge and looked down. Didn't fancy it. 'C'mon, Bambi Pavok,' I said. 'In you go.' Controversially, Bambi Pavok pulled a face. He took two steps back, moving away from the hole. What was that now. He hadn't had a problem first time around. But

Bambi Pavok didn't want to go down červí díra again. He didn't want to go back to where he'd come from. He turned to look at me with giant Bambi-eyes, built to manipulate. Now Drew took my arm, saying, don't send him back, Corey. Please reconsider. But I persisted. Ultimately, I gave Bambi Pavok a little push—.

Down he went, unceremoniously. He fell, and so did I, cognitively; that was the first revelation. Was like I could see through Bambi Pavok's eyes, hear through his ears, feel the falling sensation and the draught in his fur. He was an extension of my body going in for a white-knuckle drop – except there was nothing to hold on to, and also, no knuckles, at least where Bambi Pavok was concerned. He kept falling until he was diverted to the left, still down, but at a lesser incline. He, and me with him, in spirit, shot around bends, left again, then right, and up! The surrounding darkness segued into a pink and brown universe, refracted through, what, atmospheric turbulence, better: the transparent vortex within which we now travelled. Think abstract, think fourth-dimensional space, if not fifth, if space at all – červí díra'd be better described as a movement, perhaps, or a delirium, once you were in it. Bambi Pavok was still racing up, catapulting out of what – looking back – resembled a regular manhole. He went further up still, then ahead, hurtling down a residential street, two-storey Georgian terraces on either side. Cast-iron railings between the pavement and lower-ground-floor flats, and a tree out-side every house. Looked distinctly familiar, I thought, tumbling, catching sight of a street sign: Kalapács Road. I knew Kalapács Road. Wasn't far from Sociální Estate. The trip went abstract again, neon beige infiltration for about two or three seconds – triggering, in my view – then straight upwards, and WHACK! Bambi Pavok's flight came to an abrupt halt.

He'd crashed against a sort of provisional lid directly above him, blocking his exit. Having lost momentum, he had to work fast to achieve the required traction to keep himself up there. The alternative, to fall way back down, seemed regressive, he'd made it so far! So he clung to the sides of the vertical tunnel, le wormhole, employing the setules covering his legs, that is, millions of tiny spider-hairs with triangular tips, a wall-creeper physiology if you wish, a hang-upside-down-from-the-ceiling anatomical boon. Not quite the pickaxe principle, but do imagine like this if feels right.

On closer inspection, the proviso lid was a loosely assembled set of planks. Clinging, Bambi Pavok saw light beyond it. He heard voices. Pushing one of his frontal hooves through a gap, he tried forcing the planks apart to unblock his exit. No luck. No movement. He pushed a second foot through and tried harder. No avail. Every component part of the lid was too heavy.

Voices got louder up there. Shouting and old-fashioned swearing, who talks like that anymore. Bambi Pavok gave it one final go. He gave it his all, and yes, one of the planks moved sufficiently to create a small gap, a peephole, actually. Looking through, Bambi Pavok could confirm that above him wasn't the Forest. He was under – to apply the term loosely, conventional coordinates did not apply – one of the capital's living rooms, not now, but in the past. The fifties, or sixties, who knew. It seemed night up there, a table lamp being the main light source. Right next to červí díra, a pair of jeans and dirty white y-fronts were lying on the floor. The walls were decorated with strange collages made of cut-outs from art books and atlases. An acquired taste, not Bambi Pavok's. Cigarette smoke filled the air, and the garbage by the door could do with being taken down.

Two white guys in their thirties were involved in a domestic. Guy in Bambi Pavok's direct eyeline was wearing an ash blond wig that had moved out of position. He was in his pyjamas and in emotional pain. Talking loudly, he accused the other guy of having sex with strangers in toilets. Complained about a staggering lack of gratitude, too. About forgetting who he, the other guy, was, and who'd made him, he didn't make any sense. The accused sat on a bed above Bambi Pavok's boarded-up exit. Only his naked feet and lower legs were visible from the latter's, and my, vantage point. He barely reacted to the first guy's allegations. Let his boyfriend's anguish glide off him like it was nothing. He was numb to it all, having heard it too many times. If anything, his sporadic interjections were designed, not to connect, but to upset. Suddenly, the guy's feet disappeared from view, and the mattress springs creaked. He switched off the table lamp, letting the guy in the pyjamas know he'd had enough.

But the latter wasn't done yet. He grabbed something in the dark, what was it. A heavy object, Bambi Pavok couldn't exactly see. It emanated a strange, otherworldly light, day-glo brown on the occasion. The accuser walked towards the bed, close-up of his slippers now. He wielded the object, bringing it down, not once, not twice, but nine times in total, bludgeoning his lover, so-called, in a psychotic frenzy. When he was done, he retreated to the other side of the room, where he dropped the weapon onto the floor. He sat down at the nearby desk and deflated.

Incredibly, the victim wasn't dead. Bambi Pavok discerned laboured breathing coming from directly above. It sounded like the guy was trying to push himself off the bed. He ended up slamming onto the floor, a metre away from the boarded-up wormhole. First time Bambi Pavok, and I by extension, caught a glimpse of his face.

It was Sean. Sean St Orton, TBC television host.

He looked about ten years younger than yesterday. Besides, half his head was missing. With typical tenacity, Sean started dragging himself towards the hole in his floor, same hole that had opened up months ago inexplicably, and that he'd covered with a couple of planks, perhaps to prevent accidents. The hole would be his way out——.

Bambi Pavok understood the urgency of the situation. He decided to help. Employing two of his front legs, he tried to widen the gap between the planks a little further – no longer in order to climb out himself, but to facilitate an escape route for Sean.

Using his functioning hand, the other lay uselessly by his side, young Sean made to push the same planks out of the way——.

Bambi Pavok was labouring from below; Sean from above. Proviso lid didn't budge, their movements were cancelling each other out. Bambi Pavok didn't mean to, but was effectively blocking the dying man's exit. By the time he thought to back up, give the guy room for manoeuvre, it was too late. On the other side of the lid, Sean had stopped moving.

From the direction of the desk came the sound of a drink being poured, followed by the repeated piercing of alu foil on blister packaging. A faint smell of citrus and bitterness. Still nothing from Sean.

Clearly, most of the heavy lifting had been done:

in a last-ditch attempt, Bambi Pavok managed to push one of the planks aside, creating a gap large enough to fit through. He pulled himself up, moved his legs hectically to that end, and fell into the Kalapács Road flat in the 1960s. '67, I guessed. Pretty educated guess, I dare say.

Sean wasn't breathing. Apart from the previously white t-shirt he was wearing, he was naked. Who keeps on his t-shirt when taking his y-fronts off, Sean does. Sean did. There was blood all over the bed, the floor, the walls and even the ceiling. Bambi Pavok noticed a poster near the door advertising a couple of plays. Blood on that, too. Headshot of young Sean on it, but a different name. Not altogether different, just different. No Saint. Some sort of playwright by the looks of it, just like he'd said.

Bambi Pavok didn't know what to do with any of it. He was way out of his depth. He was already three or four, but he was young for his age. He didn't know to call emergency services, nor to alert the neighbours downstairs. He did grab the collar of Sean's t-shirt with his mouth, though, and tried to pull him down červí díra, so that he might make it to the other side, Koszmar Circus '24, the Forest '42, anywhere away from his attacker. It wasn't going so well. Sean's t-shirt kept slipping up, he was too heavy by far, and he didn't, couldn't, cooperate. Eventually, Bambi Pavok gave up.

On the '24 side of things, I was watching. Was like I existed simultaneously here, Koszmar Circus in '24, and Kalapács Road in '67. I held my hand out to Drew which they took. 'Corey?' they said. 'What's happening?'

Bambi Pavok spied the perpetrator folded over the desk next to half a glass of grapefruit juice and an empty box of Nembutal tablets: a sedative which in high doses caused respiratory arrest, I'd later gather. Wig resting on the side of his face like a bird's nest, he was barely conscious and no longer posing a threat. Curiously, Bambi Pavok stepped closer. Stacks of paper, notebooks and a mechanical typewriter on the desk. Dirty plates, too, with traces of what looked like a meal consisting of rice and tinned fish, and more rice, with golden syrup. There was that otherworldly light again. Where did it come from? There, on the floor, by the perp's slippers. A trophy, of all things, day-glo brown in this instance, now with a bloody sheen. Said 'Award for the Dramatisation of Social Evils 1967' on it. As far as murder weapons went, a theatrical choice.

I heard sirens draw closer through Bambi Pavok's sensitive ears. Struck me it wouldn't look good to an outsider, that is, Bambi Pavok and a murder-suicide. He really ought to get out of there before the police arrived. Sirens were getting louder. In a minute, police would be outside and then inside the flat. The TBC might turn up. Young Sean was a public figure, wasn't he? What if the camera crew was already downstairs. Bambi Pavok, what can you see?!

Bambi Pavok rushed to the window. Two police cars drew up at the kerb. Four, five officers, filing out and into the house. Steps coming up the stairs.

'Police! Open the door!'

Run, Bambi Pavok. Run, don't look back. Červí díra? Back down you go—.

'POLICE! OPEN THE DOOR! ONE. TWO—.'

But Bambi Pavok didn't go down the wormhole, not just yet. He turned round and looked back over the room. The day-glo brown trophy lay on the floor. So Bambi Pavok did a detour. He went over. Don't know why he did it, I didn't tell him to. He brought out his embarrassment, his forbidden mouthpart, and proceeded to plant it against St Orton's trophy. He applied suction.

'THREE!' Police started to break down the door.

Bambi Pavok, little sucker – don't like to use bottom-shaming language but was what it was – lifted and carried, weaving, the dead playwright's trophy towards červí díra. He went down just as the police barged their way in, as ever infiltrating gay personal spaces when it was too late by far.

For Bambi Pavok, it could go either way at this

point. Koszmar Circus '24, the Forest '42, and who knew what other exits existed. Malachi Hölderlin's bathroom sink – remember? Florida Rot part of town? I didn't know how it worked exactly, but it'd become clear that červí díra organisation was far more complex than the Sean of the *Gets to the Bottom of It* era had accounted for. I'd tell him, too, I thought, that his theory wasn't all that. I'd not get the chance to, but I didn't know that yet.

After a trip down several vertical loops, Bambi Pavok tumbled out at the sylvan end of affairs. It wasn't until he found himself lying face down on green moss, legs akimbo, surrounded by common spruces and giant sequoia trees, that he let go of St Orton's trophy. Once he released suction, it rolled down a gentle slope and into a shallow ditch, where it lay like a squandered opportunity.

8

Frikadellen, best in Forest.

Four, five weeks after Bambi Pavok's departure: was the part of the Forest in 1942 that looked like a fast-food restaurant by the side of a motorway in a left-behind Euro country circa 1999. A small pond with oil slick on top out front. Landscaped greenery strewn with rubbish, and a few forlorn picnic tables. Inside, Drew was at the counter ordering a veggie burger. They didn't have that. They had frikadellen in this hinterland shack. Venison frikadellen, to be exact, locally sourced. That's what the server, in a fetching pink-brown uniform including cap with red writing on it, said to Drew, matter-of-factly. Was False Widower of the Forest on shift at his latest job, which, if history was anything to go by, he wouldn't last in beyond a couple of months tops. He was handling six frying pans simultaneously, also blindly, that is, behind his back, while operating the cash register with his remaining appendages, serving Drew. Next to the cooker, a large electric meat grinder was ON, evidencing the freshly preparedness of the day's frikadellen, making a whirring noise.

'Alright, I'll have three,' Drew said. Unusual, Drew being vegetarian. They studied the backlit menu above the counter. 'Also, French fries and Mezzo Mix. Largest you got.' Drew turned round to our table, where TBC camera operator Uwe and myself were waiting, giving the ok sign. A paper ice-bucket branded 'Frikadellen, Best in Forest' came over the counter, containing a litre of fizzy pop.

Drew had been the one who'd thought the idea of going Forest worth pursuing. Actually, they'd insisted we'd go. They still hadn't given up on me retrieving, if not *the* trophy, then *a* trophy, and presenting it to Social Evils and whoever else wanted to see it, the wider public. I'd *won*, they'd said, and I should have something to show for it. If the particular exemplar we'd set eyes on most recently had belonged to Sean St Orton, or whatever his name had been when he'd received it, so be it. To Drew's mind, the least we could do for Sean was to give his trophy another life. After all, we had, not just technically killed him in '67, but as it'd turned out, disappeared him from the present. Drew was convinced that the two were related, cause-and-effect type scenario. Sending Bambi Pavok to Kalapács Road, blocking emergency exit, we'd created a version of the past in which Sean didn't – *couldn't*, in fact – escape through červí díra, which'd had implications for the present. With Sean gone, his trophy was all we had left of him, and given my recent role as his *replacement*—. Drew'd stopped in mid-sentence. I, Corey, owed this to Sean, they'd concluded, and to them, Drew. To us, our relationship, and even to Bambi Pavok. 'Give him a chance to redeem himself. If nothing else, he'll have helped collect trophy.'

Personally, I'd been reluctant to go Forest for a variety of deeply repressed historical reasons. Besides, I was done with trophy collection, and I mean *done*. During the two weeks that had passed since Drew's and my noncommittal visit to the Prokletý Field production site that had ended with my recruitment, I'd as good as done away with any conception I'd had of myself as award-winning novelist. I'd be going into tv, and that was that. Tv would be better for me. But what had happened was, I'd let slip that Bambi Pavok had returned to the Forest for good, was how I'd phrased it. Hearing this, the TBC had made a travel budget available and insisted I go Forest ASAP, to record a trailer for *Corey Fah Does Social Mobility* 'in the field'. 'Commit top boy on film,' the showrunner had insisted. Make the most of it, fieldwork was not about to become the norm. For the remainder of the series I'd be stuck in Prokletý Field stadium. As if that was a hardship, the showrunner had laughed. What a location, ey, Corey Fah. Elbow in ribs.

Early this morning, Drew, Uwe and I had travelled to the Forest in '42 via Koszmar Circus červí díra. We were careful to avoid Kalapács Road '67 exit, arriving at our destination without any incidents. First impressions, the Forest was as sublime and overwhelming as it was strangely uniform: high fir trees, pines, repeat ad nauseam. We experienced absurdly high oxygen levels. Disappointingly, we weren't able to locate Sean's trophy in the ditch where I'd seen Bambi Pavok drop it. We searched the area, which proved a challenge on account of the extreme monotony of the environment. One tree after another, Drew complained at one point. Trees, trees, trees, trees. Did we come past here before? Minutes ago? I didn't know. What I did know was, no sign of the trophy. Nor, for that matter, Bambi Pavok. Apropos the latter: he would've been back half a day at this point, whereas for us, he'd left weeks ago. I tried tuning in with him, see through his eyes, identify landmarks that indicated his approximate location. But all I was able to discern was the bottom half of a small, untidy office space. For reasons I didn't understand, the upper half of my visual was blacked out. Primarily, I made out a moss-green carpet, the legs of a desk, a plant pot, and a bunch of large deer hooves between the plastic wheels of an office chair. Didn't make any sense, so I stopped that. Reception must be bad in the Forest, I told myself. Never mind. At this point, the smell of cooking drifted into the woods, a welcome distraction. Drew, Uwe and I agreed we deserved a break. We walked until we discovered a motorway which we followed. It was littered with roadkill on either side. How relieved we were when we spotted the brightly coloured fast-food restaurant at the Forest's edge.

Drew was meaning to drop their change into the, what, day-glo brown tip jar on the counter. As their hand approached, the tip jar inched back of its own accord. Drew tried again. Same reaction.

'What's that tip jar you got there on the counter,' Drew asked.

'Oh that old thing,' sang the False Widower. He'd found it in a ditch this morning, lying on its side. It'd been filthy, but he'd cleaned it nice.

'It belongs to my friend.' Drew said 'friend', not 'lover' or 'life partner', as was advisable given the provincial and trans-historical properties of this particular part of the Forest.

'Does it.' False Widower took his pans off the cooker. He crossed several sets of arms in front of his chest, staring down Drew.

'It does.'

'Says who.'

'It's got their name on it, literally. Corey Fah. See?'

'Says O-R-T-O-N.'

'What I meant.'

At the table, I did my best to disappear.

'Tell him, he can come and get it,' False Widower said to Drew. 'See what happens.'

Reluctantly, I got up and went to the counter. 'I can hear you, you know,' I said to False Widower. Behind me, I heard Uwe unzip the camera bag. He'd be filming the confrontation, was what he was here for. First bit of action since we'd arrived in the sticks.

'And who we got here,' the False Widower said, scrutinising me.

'Corey Fah, award-winning author.'

Award-winning, huh? I didn't look it. Matter of fact, I looked like a foreigner, coming here, telling the locals what and what not was theirs to own.

'Trophy is mine,' I said in the exact local dialect. 'You can keep it though.'

Trophy, what trophy. False Widower rejected the assumption that the object on his counter was a trophy. Didn't look like one, shy and retiring thing. Not that it'd been hard to catch, if you had eight arms and legs, that is. Made for a decent tip jar to his mind. He'd keep it, I was right about that. No thanks to me.

'Where's your complaints box,' Drew asked.

I noticed a large poster on the wall depicting a twelve-pointer stag. It was the Great Prince of the Forest, original Bambi-father, looking majestic against fir-green background. One of his front hooves was raised, and gently placed onto a venison burger on the pine-needle-carpeted floor in front of him. 'Frikadellen, Best in Forest' was written at the bottom, right. Odd,

I thought. Not many households in the Forest had pictures of the Great Prince on the wall, or at least they didn't use to, and certainly none involving branded food stuff.

On the counter, the trophy got testy as its surroundings got lively, what else was new. It lifted off its regular spot and glided backwards, until it hovered directly above the electric meat grinder. A day-glo brown catch-me-if-you-can situation, if ever I saw one.

'Come here and get it, Corey Fah,' False Widower taunted. 'Tell you what – if you can get it, you can keep it.'

What's wrong with him, starting up again. I'd already said I didn't want it. But Uwe was pointing his camera at me, encouraging me.

'Go on, Corey, let's have at it,' Uwe said. Don't let him treat you like this. Who's he to you anyway? Let's see some action, make the field trip worthwhile. Scoreboard at Prokletý Field isn't slowing down, either. Remember the scoreboard? Tick tock, Corey Fah. Tick tock.

'What is it,' False Widower said. 'You scared?'

This could go one of several ways, I thought. I could act on my sense of injustice, remember everything that had been withheld from me starting from young, and go for it. Or I could play to the camera, commit to content creation, for Uwe, for Sean, for the

TBC, for the writer I'd worked so hard to become, and for my new television host self. I could push myself off the counter, and use the momentum to bounce off False Widower's chest, sending him backwards into the giant meat grinder. Falling, he might employ one of his many appendages to snare me, taking me — and if I'd snatched it, the trophy — down with him. Le mincemeat, the end. Or, I could refuse to be roped into False Widower's insidious game, what a concept. Realising that non-participation was an option available to me felt like a privilege. Hadn't always been the case.

'No thanks,' I said to False Widower. 'As a tv presenter, I've no use for a trophy.' Wave to the camera, old man. Once my show would go out next month — in circa eighty-two years to you, or, if the 1999 affectation was anything to go by, in twenty-five — I'd be known internationally. Regular face on television screens everywhere, including the former territories of the Soviet Union I bet. 'Do you get TBC One round here?' I asked.

Yeah he didn't watch it. He only watched Forest One and FTV5.

A loud and distorted voice came through the intercom, 'Any problemy down there?'

'No, boss. No problemy.' False Widower got one of his arms in gear, wiping down the work surface behind him, looking busy. He used another arm to flip a frikadelle, all the while continuing to intimidate me.

'Good. I've got the new washer-upper up here——.' The transmission ended with a click.

I could've just left it and walked out. For all intents and purposes, I'd won. But I didn't, walk out – continuing a running theme, I failed to capitalise on a win. 'Who was that,' I asked instead. And what washer-upper was he referring to. I'd noticed a disconcertingly large stack of dirty dishes next to a sink. Industrial dishwasher next to it, sign fitted saying 'out of order'.

Was bossman, according to the False Widower. Frikadellen, Best in Forest was owned by the Great Prince of the Forest, now going by the name of Great Prince-boss of the Fast-Food Restaurant. Great Prince-boss's MO was putting his own people through the grinder, letting them feed on each other, while casually running a profit. He'd had a surveillance system installed, False Widower continued, allowing him to watch and listen in on the restaurant from his office upstairs. False Widower contorted his face into a smile for the camera – not Uwe's, CCTV. I watched him deploy all eight appendages just to stay on top of his workload, thinking, You, big man, are just as oppressed as everyone else.

I requested to speak to the Great Prince-boss of the Fast-Food Restaurant.

False Widower, who'd been squirting mustard onto three half-built burgers, stopped in mid-movement. He proceeded to lean forward onto the counter in a confrontational manner. 'Boss,' he said to the room, not taking his eyes off me. 'Customer wants to talk to you.'

Intercom remained silent.

'That's a no, Corey Fah.' The False Widower relaxed his stare and went back to adding pickled gherkins, cut length-wise, to his work in progress. Finally, he placed three perfect burgers in pink-brown cartons, red logos on them, on top of the counter. 'Trays and paper napkins over there.'

'Tell him about the tv crew,' I said, pointing at Uwe. 'TBC One!' I called into the intercom.

Painfully loud crackling and a distorted voice saying, 'I'll be down.'

Well, well, how about that. First time I'd used my newly acquired social status as person with access to my advantage. No one says no to free publicity.

The staircase shook as the Great Prince-boss of the Fast-Food Restaurant came down and burst through a small door at the bottom. He was in a brown suit jacket, too tight across his broad shoulders. Frikadellen, Best in Forest pin on his lapel. 'Where's the camera,' he asked, proceeding to replicate his pose from the poster, sans burger.

The Great Prince-boss's impressive entrance was somewhat marred by someone tripping, it seemed, then falling down the staircase behind him. Why was I not surprised to see Bambi Pavok tumbling out of the open door. He slid bottom-first through the stag's legs and came to a halt in front of the counter. He was wearing, or trying to wear, the Frikadellen-branded cap. Several sizes too large, it had slid over the top four of his eyes, impacting his vision. Instead of the regular uniform, he was kitted out in a pink-brown trainee t-shirt, size XXL. From under his cap, bewildered, Bambi Pavok looked at Uwe the camera op. Noticing Drew and myself, his eyes opened, wide, wider, the bottom row, then reduced to a squint. Chin in the air, he slowly, deliberately, turned his head in the opposite direction. Clearly, he wasn't talking to us.

I looked at Drew, raising an eyebrow. We'd taken the fact that Bambi Pavok had collected Sean's trophy when given the chance as a sign that he'd wanted to redeem himself, which would imply that he'd forgiven us for sending him back. This wasn't the case.

'False Widower,' Great Prince-boss of the Fast-Food Restaurant said. 'Here's your new washer-upper. He just got the job. Use him as you see fit.' The stag pushed Bambi Pavok in the behind, insisting he get busy and familiarise himself with his new workplace. 'Off you go, Bambi Pavok. See the dishes by the side of the sink? Get at it. No need to be shy.'

Bambi Pavok got up and made his way to what would be his spot for the foreseeable, and where the wasteman that was his father and latterly line manager was waiting for him. He kept tripping over the hem of his t-shirt which was sweeping the floor.

'Wipe that look off your face,' False Widower said, seeing his prodigal son whose absence he hadn't noticed – for one, because, technically, no time at all had passed since the latter's departure. But in the space of no time at all, Bambi Pavok had developed a know-it-all, quasi-urbane facial expression which hadn't been there this morning. False Widower couldn't specify what exact changes he was registering, but he didn't like them one bit. 'Start on that,' he said, pushing Bambi Pavok towards the sink, putting him right in his place.

The new employee got up on his hind legs, ran the tap, and tackled the dishes with the filthy sponge and the heavy-duty washing-up liquid. Within seconds, his t-shirt was wet.

What's that shitty thing hovering over his meat grinder, the Great Prince-boss of the Fast-Food Restaurant asked. Was it flesh fly? Would the False Widower see to the shit fly being removed, stat. The dishwasher could do it.

'Is a day-glo brown flesh fly,' I confirmed, drawing attention to myself, arguably unnecessarily. Was all it was. Into the kitchen waste with it, see if I cared. Uwe went in on a close-up of my face, to see if I really believed what I was saying.

That was it, Drew'd had enough. Don't think they'd forgiven me for what I'd done to Bambi Pavok and, inevitably, Sean St Orton. Don't think they condoned me calling Sean's trophy a shit fly, and, more to the point, refusing to even try to collect it despite the fact it was within reach. Never assume they'd accepted my participation in the programme of Sean's substitution, and yet, what riled them the most was this camera op – Uwe – exploiting the situation, and me in it, for cheap television content. Despite everything, Drew felt protective over me, a pattern that'd been established way back in '03, when we first met. They walked up behind Uwe. They could've asked him to stop filming, please, and to observe people's – my – privacy in critical moments, but they didn't. They poured what was left of their Mezzo Mix over Uwe's camera, effectively putting it out of action. As I said, they'd been a little unmoored lately. Multiple stresses. Blood sugar spike didn't help.

'Ah, what! TBC property?!' Uwe inspected the camera briefly, declared it ruined and came for Drew. 'You know what one of these costs?'

Great Prince-boss of the Fast-Food Restaurant didn't have time for any of it, especially now that the possibility of a tv appearance had effectively disappeared. He had a business to run. Global expansion plans to pursue. 'Take it outside,' he told Uwe and

Drew, in no uncertain terms. Fighting wasn't tolerated in here.

'We're not leaving without Bambi Pavok,' Drew said, bravely.

Despite moving a lot, the former had barely made a dent in his stack of dishes. He'd also flooded his work area, which I knew because my trainers felt wet vicariously.

Great Prince-boss of the Fast-Food Restaurant moved himself between us and his new washer-upper. Everything in Frikadellen burger bar and, for that matter, the Forest, was his, as far as he was concerned. He threw his head down, presenting his antlers, and said, 'Get out. All of you.' He took a step forwards.

'Bambi Pavok!' Drew called, retreating. 'Let's go, let's go!'

Having heard Drew perfectly well, Bambi Pavok pretended he hadn't. He didn't have the emotional maturity to get over himself at this critical juncture, preferring to focus on washing dishes, making his point. He'd rather stay in the Forest for good than snap out of his pique fit. Plus, he didn't dare run past the Great Prince-boss of the Fast-Food Restaurant, who'd skewer him, for all he knew.

The stag advanced again, wielding his twelve-pointer aggressively. Grunting, he started charging. Drew, Uwe and I left in a hurry.

On route back to červí díra, Drew was silent. Uwe wasn't talkative either. I was eating my frikadelle on the go. Get any good shots, Uwe? Material we can use? Was quite something, I continued, seeing Bambi Pavok in his natural habitat, reunited with his biological father, engaging in lowly paid child labour. Almost touching, I said, to see him resume the path in life that'd always been his.

Drew looked at me. 'Honestly, Corey.' They didn't think any of it particularly touching, no. Matter of fact, the Forest was worse than they'd imagined. Bambi Pavok's working environment? Toxic. They considered . . . *this*, all of it, Uwe, the Great Prince-boss, the False Widower, the worst possible outcome. *Fuck*.

In many ways, Drew was expressing what I was feeling but tried very hard not to. Why were they like that. Always challenging me. Always calling out my BS.

9

Malachi Hölderlin returns as avenging angel.

First thing I noticed walking into Prokletý Field stadium was a general nervousness among staff. No one looked me in the eye. Technicians, runners, camera operators stood in circles, putting their heads together, whispering, gesticulating, dispersing when I approached. Anyone gonna tell me what's going on? Oh. The scoreboard. Instead of 6,906 hours, that is, the number of hours in a prize year minus the number of hours in the eleven weeks that had passed since my win, it displayed one (1) hour, some thirty-three minutes and forty-four seconds. Forty-three. Forty-two. What's that supposed to mean. Felt malicious, as far as communications went. As if my time was running out rather sooner than I'd expected. Were we dealing with a technical error? Wear and tear on account of the age of the thing, its dubious provenance, preposterous size and long-term exposure to acid rain? Unless a person did this. Anyone, fix it?

Social Evils had agreed to reteleport despite their reservations. Almost two weeks – or nine episodes – into the inaugural run of *Corey Fah Does Social Mobility*, the plan was to pull out the stops for the tenth. Personally,

I'd voted against reteleportation, even for the expressed purpose of content creation for live tv – as persuasive a rationale, as valid a motivation, as any. As I said, I was done chasing neon beige Moby Dick. I'd entered into a state of acceptance. I'd moved on with my life, which in itself presented a problem insofar as it showed on tv. Central conceit of the series dictated that I looked like I cared. Following pressure from the showrunner, I'd agreed to play along and fake it for the camera. They'd go through with reteleportation, and I'd put my soul into securing the trophy like I used to. I'd try very hard to do social mobility in the exact way I was expected to, promised. 'Good,' the showrunner had said. Increasingly, I was losing sight of who I was, and that's saying something, given the extent to which I'd been in the dark in the first place.

On the pitch, near the west curve of the stadium, a small square base – a plinth – had been prepared: covered with a purple and grey zigzaggy tablecloth in honour of the original host, it constituted a mini landing pad for the trophy. Once the latter arrived over Prokletý Field, it should find its way there, Social Evils prize coordinator had agreed. To the right of the plinth, Sean's original swivel chairs had been positioned. They seemed lost to their savage environment. Still no one cut the grass? Anyone? But staff were visibly busy. Seemed like I was the only one standing around without purpose.

Almost eleven weeks after first going on, Malachi Hölderlin – the sad quasi-adolescent of previous *St Orton Gets to the Bottom of It* fame – would be back by popular demand. I'd been informed that she'd arrived an hour ago and that she'd been taken to make-up. She'd come alone, that is, without her pet bunny.

The TBC had been quick to resurrect the show's original interview format, or a version of it. In practice, the writers' room had proven too expensive, labour-intensive and time-consuming. (Had affected the spontaneity and liveness of the show detrimentally, went the official line; also, some continuity wasn't a bad thing.) Whereas 'revisited' was as cheap as tv formats came, Drew'd pointed out, rightly. Today, Malachi and I would sit and chat. I'd follow up with her, get the low-down on her deranged rabbit. The talk element would segue into the action part of the show, involving me, Corey Fah, doing social mobility. I'd wait for the trophy to come into view and extemporise, to an extent. Do my thing, apparently, and do it to camera.

'Thirty minutes until we go live!' the director announced through a megaphone, *Gets to* sticker still on it. 'Anyone going to fix the scoreboard?' I asked. 'Before we commit the corrupted data to film?'

'What's that you got there,' I asked a passing technician. She was carrying a pink-brown burger-size carton, red logo on it. A franchise, Frikadellen, Best in Town, had opened its first restaurant in the capital, she said, and a kiosk on site. See over there? Official partner of the TBC. Want to try? Is delicious. I did not, want to try. I saw what she meant, though. A small Frikadellen outlet, a pinkish kiosk, had appeared near the ex-players'-tunnel like a gash in the terrace. I was surprised they'd opened an outlet solely for the television crew and the small number of guests. Despite or because of the stadium's large capacity, the live audience element had been scrapped as part of the relaunch.

Ah! Carrying an unusually elongated gym bag, Malachi Hölderlin was marching across the playing field towards me. Her oversized Bela Lugosi's Dead t-shirt flapped in the wind as she came closer. Worth mentioning that the weather had been heinous all day. Purple clouds hurtled across a pink and beige sky, displaying a tendency to gather over the stadium. I offered my hand, how are you. Malachi just glared at me, saying nothing. What's *her* problem, I thought. She nervous about the interview? Hadn't seemed like it last time round. Did she resent me for not being Sean? Many people did, latterly. Malachi didn't know anything about me, I thought – as it'd turn out: wrongly – other than that I wasn't Sean. She dropped her bag by her chair and sat down.

Sound technician fitted us with headsets, then

switched on the control monitor in front of us. Two camera operators strapped on their Steadicams, trying out possible angles. If the chairs were in the foreground, the lifetime scoreboard needed to remain visible in the background, was the requirement. Behind them, another crew member was testing a camera crane, enabling hundred-and-twenty-degree sweeps if desired. For the latter part of the show, the crew had a drone at the ready. It lay on the ground like a resting insect.

Malachi and I were in position, facing each other. I nodded and smiled, doing all the emotional labour required of a television host. Nothing came back. She dead inside.

'Thirty seconds,' the director announced.

Malachi bent down and unzipped her bag. She pulled out a semi-automatic assault rifle which she proceeded to point at my chest. Price sticker of the international supermarket still on the magazine.

'Abort,' the director whispered into his mic. 'Do not go live. I repeat, abort.'

Malachi overheard and wielded her rifle like a stag might his antlers. She demanded we broadcast as planned. 'Don't try anything,' she said to the director. 'Goes for you, too, Corey Fah. We're doing this.' Five, four, one—.

We were live. Framing shot of the stadium, centring the hostage situation: Malachi with Kalashnikov, myself, targeted, holding on to the armrests of my chair. Behind us, the scoreboard was swaying precariously, counting twenty-eight minutes and thirty-eight seconds. Thirty-seven. Thirty-six. The wind picked up, getting caught in our clothes, our hair, our microphones.

'Viewers,' I said, to camera. 'We're live from Prokletý Field stadium, home to *Corey Fah Does Social Mobility*. Special show today, as you can see. Not for the faint-hearted. You might recognise Malachi Hölderlin from *Florida Rot*, former guest on *St Orton Gets to the Bottom of It*. Who could forget her, or her time-travelling rabbit! I hope you will join me in welcoming Malachi, with Kalashnikov on the occasion. So, Malachi. How have you been since we last saw you on tv. How is your pet? He didn't come?'

The clouds drifted apart. Starting from the east curve of the stadium, a stretch of sunlight travelled across Prokletý Field including Malachi and myself, our desperate, diminutive scenario.

'How have I been, Corey Fah? How do *you* think I've been.'

Ok, I didn't get a good feeling.

'How do you think my bunny has been – Fumper.'

Fumper. I was getting a worse feeling still. Evidently, Malachi was harbouring deeper resentments than first I'd realised. I tried to think of something to say that might diffuse the situation. But what.

'Nothing, Corey Fah? Really? I'll tell you how I've been. See what you think,' Malachi said, cynically. Then she launched into the following:

After her appearance on *Gets to*, Malachi had dropped out of uni. Having been told by Sean in no uncertain terms that she'd be on her own, she'd seen no other way than to fully dedicate herself to the project of getting to the bottom of it, if viewers at home would indulge her and allow the retired phrase. She'd needed to know what exactly had happened to Fumper, what physically and psychologically had done him in, and, by extension, herself. Otherwise the uncertainty would've eaten her alive, she knew what she was like. She had analytical brain so she'd tracked Fumper's moves retrospectively. Here's what she'd concluded – a trajectory of a sad little life, ultimately cut short.

Malachi was able to confirm that Fumper had indeed crawled out of červí díra, that is, the drain of her bathroom sink, in 2014, like she'd suspected. She didn't know where he'd come from originally – some enchanted Forest she'd like to imagine, where deer ran free and rabbits got twitterpated. Didn't know how she knew, intuition. But when Fumper'd gone AWOL first time around? Before she'd come on *Gets to*? Nothing to do with červí díra, she now believed. Instead, he'd broken out of his cage, made for the first-floor window of Malachi's bedroom, dived down and proceeded to fend for his life in the swamp behind Florida Rot apartment block. Didn't bear thinking about what had happened to him in that swamp. Destitute place, characterised by waterlogged greenery and unnatural flowers secreting a distinct iron-y smell – the ultimate giveaway. Remember, he'd smelled iron-y on return? Invisible snakes lived in that swamp. Disembodied eye-balls with bat wings lived there, eyeballs with retractable eye-stalks, like, a set of snail tentacles periscoping you whichever way you turned, and eyeballs with lightning bolts for legs, all of them, *all* of them, out to destroy you. No wonder Fumper had returned with his head hanging off to the left, it wouldn't stay up straight, and a whole set of behavioural problems. He'd always had a belligerent streak, but not like that. Anyway, Malachi believed that after eleven days in the swamp he'd clawed his way out and up the staircase of her block. He'd waited by the door to her apartment, number thirteen, he was smart like that. After sitting for hours, he'd slipped in behind her mother who'd been returning from work. He'd slithered into the bathroom where he'd sat on the cold white tiles, creature of habit, until she, Malachi, had found him eventually.

What you think about this, though, Corey Fah, Malachi continued. Two days after she'd been on *St Orton*

Gets to the Bottom of It, Fumper had only been back, what, a couple of weeks, he'd disappeared *again*. Her window had been closed, sealed, if I wished, blinds nailed down and gaffer-taped – precautions she'd taken following Fumper's foray into the swamp. By process of elimination, Malachi'd concluded that, for the second time in his life, he'd taken a trip through červí díra. He'd gone down the drain for real this time, though previously, in '14, he'd come up it, of course. Did I, Corey Fah, know what that even did to you, the constant coming and going? The blowing hot, then cold? She'd made an active decision to save herself, disinvest and forget about Fumper. It would be better for everyone if he'd stay away. Hadn't been her baby anymore anyway, just a rabid, one-toothed, yellow-eyed caricature of his former self. 'I let go, Corey Fah. I was starting to feel almost normal.' So, imagine how she'd felt when——. Malachi couldn't believe when she'd seen her bunny, her Fumper, on what would turn out to be the last-ever episode of *St Orton Gets to the Bottom of It*: the one in which I, Corey Fah, had been the guest. Fumper's appearance had been brief, brutal and ill-fated. But I knew that. Malachi knew that I knew that. As far as she was concerned, I was personally responsible, not just for Fumper's death, but the violent manner in which it'd occurred. Was my job to control my, what was it, even, like a Staffy or a pit bull, but thin. Slender, eight-legged. Was my time to pay up now. To make reparation for what

I'd done to Fumper, and, consequently, Malachi herself. This, here, was how she'd achieve closure.

She took aim at my heart, I supposed. Rough area.

'Don't,' I said. 'Go live a life, Malachi. Find a friend or a lover. Isn't there anyone you like? Alternatively, stay single, very good, too. Develop an obsession, you obviously have it in you.' My thoughts were racing: two days after Malachi's appearance on final *Gets to* – it tracked. What if there *was* červí díra between Florida Rot apartment block and Koszmar Circus – Fumper could have been there for twitterpation, complete with pathological behaviour. No time travel involved on the occasion, just a spatial leap, so to speak, at least on his part – his friends and lover would've come from the Forest, the past, a trans-historical rendezvous. Who knew how červí díry worked anyway, or what variations existed. I, for one, had a couple of working theories, but largely, I was overextended. Takeaway being, Drew's Fumper was Malachi's. Correction: *had been*.

'I don't have a life,' Malachi replied. She'd once had a bunny, that was it. Was just her and her semi-automatic now.

Someone detached from the stands. Through the wasteland of Prokletý Field, this angel, a civilian, was walking towards us, taking an incalculable risk. As they came nearer, I saw they were wearing a brand-new bomber jacket. A washed-out sweater and familiar pink tracksuit bottoms. Drew, I thought. Not Drew. Don't let it be Drew. Last thing I wanted was them in the firing line.

Noticing the change in my expression, Malachi pivoted around. 'Drew!' Her voice went up at the sight of Drew. Later, she'd explain that she'd seen them on live tv after their rabbit, *her* rabbit, had died at the hands – the mouthpart – of Bambi Pavok. There'd been a revealing close-up of Drew, they'd been devastated. Malachi had seen her own feelings reflected in this Drew character's face. You can't fake that sort of thing. So Malachi trusted Drew. She thought she could talk with them. She suspected they'd looked after Fumper very well until he'd been taken from them, and from her, so cruelly, so prematurely.

'Hi Malachi. Put down your weapon? How about it,' Drew said, hands in their jogger pockets. This was the Drew I knew, good at de-escalation. Not erratic like latterly. Not reactive, but composed.

'Did he suffer?' Fumper.

'He did.'

'What you do with his body, what was left of it?'

'Carried it home in a plastic bag. Buried it under a patch of daisies on estate. Want to come visit? Light a candle? Leave some flowers?'

Fumper had loved a swamp-dwelling violet, actually, with its fleshy leaves and barbaric appetites. 'Alright,' Malachi said. 'I'll visit.'

'Oh good. Assault rifle? Give it here?' Drew took a step towards Malachi.

She deliberated, then shrugged. Butt-first, she handed Drew the Kalashnikov.

The crew breathed out noticeably, whereas I felt only partial relief. It didn't make sense that Malachi should relent that easily, given the strength of her feeling and the amount of planning that would've gone into avenging Fumper. Way she'd handed over her rifle had felt more hey-ho, what do I care, rather than repentant in any way. My suspicion wasn't unfounded: when Drew wasn't looking, Malachi turned to me, mouthing, watch your back, Corey Fah. Don't think you'll get away lightly. Was she telling me she had something else in store? Something bigger?

I saw it on the control monitor first: as if on cue, the trophy came into view. It came out of the sky behind Malachi and me, homing in on its bespoke landing pad. Drew saw it, too.

As my nemesis moved through the atmosphere, contrails appeared in its wake. Not the typical line-shaped streamers a plane might produce, but rather a series of malevolent fluff-balls. White initially, they quickly turned purple, increasing in volume. The first lightning bolts were almost innocent-looking, like cartoon abstractions. But soon after, significant weather events were unleashed, same genre as Florida Rot swamp animals. Eyeballs with bat wings and additional eye-stalks released lightning bolts at a rat-a-tat rate. Rain poured out of their collective tear ducts and onto Prokletý Field including us.

As the UFO continued its approach – the flying object remained unidentifiable to me in the deepest possible sense – the winds picked up way beyond their usual force and velocity, blowing east. The trophy pushed towards the plinth, its top ahead of its body. But the more it put into it, the more harrowing the lightning storm became. Enormous cumulonimbus clouds like purple continents formed over the stadium, as a next-level gust lifted plastic seats clear out of their fixtures and into the air. Discarded Frikadellen, Best in Town cartons went flying like leaves. There – a freak bolt hit the scoreboard. The latter's hardware changed colour from black to maroon, the digits turning day-glo. The countdown sped up, just a fraction – eleven minutes and thirty-one seconds. Thirty. Twenty-nine. Circa a hundred metres away from Drew, Malachi and me, the trophy got stuck in mid-air. Forces of its own making, it seemed, were moving against it.

I knew what was going to happen before it did. As I said, I'd been working on a couple of theories, this was one: what if there was a link between the movement of cultural capital and the emergence of červí díry. In other words, what if červí díry were an unintended consequence of teleporting trophies from their regular place in the ideological depot, the cultural-capital supernatural hoard, to a landing port, Koszmar Circus, or Prokletý Field, right here on Earth.

There it was. The ground started to tremble, subtly at first. Parts of the stadium's roof structure snapped and crashed into what was left of the stands. Then the entirety of the former playing field started subsiding, slowly initially, then building into a seismic drop. I'd predicted it: a giant červí díra opened, like hell-mouth, like something absolutely uncontained and overwhelmingly devastating.

If reteleportation was needed, that is, if for whatever reason normal collection wasn't achieved, if the winner fluffed it, the risk of the spatiotemporal continuum caving in increased exponentially. Laid the risk firmly with recipients who didn't know shit about collecting prizes; who didn't have anyone in their extended social circle who did; who hadn't had the right sort of training, like Sean St Orton or myself. Certainly looked like it from where I stood – on increasingly dodgy ground, to be fair.

Last thing the tv crew did, was to launch the camera drone. As Malachi, Drew, the confiscated Kalashnikov, the supercharged scoreboard, the iconic swivel chairs and the crew themselves were going down, it broadcast the aerial view: the ruin of the stadium and what remained of the pink plastic seats would be enough to give the impression of an actual orifice, a literal hell-mouth, if you like. The image live viewers would've been left with would've been the scoreboard, I imagined, falling, counting down, ten minutes and five seconds, four seconds, three, until it, too, would've disappeared. Me, Corey Fah? I raced to the bottom more persuasively than before, taking everybody down with me.

10

Corey Fah wouldn't mind if they never entered another time loop in their life.

Where were we. Still Prokletý Field stadium, but not as we left it. For starters, the ground was back in place. Drew, Malachi, myself and the various crew members were lying on it – bewildered, disoriented, but seemingly intact. Drew? Drew! You ok? They gave me the ok sign which I returned. The trophy lay next to its plinth on the floor, zigzag tablecloth on it like a blanket. Let's hope we put that to bed, I thought, optimistically, or cynically, who's to say. Unusually, the sun was shining. The sky was blue. What was that, though, structural changes to the stadium itself. Instead of the regular stands, Sociální Estate was bordering on the playing field to the east. Was like it had been transported from Huàirén to Prokletý Field in its entirety, dismantled and rebuilt, perhaps, brick by brick. Drew got up and walked over to me, their joggers torn at the seat. Their left elbow was chafed. What is this, they asked, meaning everything. The entire north side of the stands, and this hurt, was filled with row upon row of Frikadellen, Best in Town outlets. From left to right, bottom to top, staggered, there were hundreds of them: le Frikadellen village, distinctly pink-brown-and-red-branded. Small comfort was, all of their front shutters were currently closed. What else. Several familiar sceneries had materialised along the edge of the pitch, and some on it. Drew, are you seeing this? To our right, several identical studio remakes of the Great Prince-boss of the Fast-Food Restaurant's office space had been lined up. I'd only ever seen the bottom half through Bambi Pavok's eyes, but I recognised that moss-green carpet, the particular plant pot, the base of that desk and the plastic wheels of the chair when I saw them – on the occasion, times six or seven. Perplexingly, there was a stag, *thee* stag, the Great Prince-boss of the Fast-Food Restaurant, in each of the workplace scenarios. Each of them sat on his respective chair doing paperwork, apart from the one on the left who displayed classic stress pattern weaving in his enclosure. No scoreboard in this version of Prokletý Field as far as I could tell. I thought that progressive.

With some concern, I noticed that the tv crew weren't filming any of it. The live broadcast of the show must've been disrupted when we'd gone down červí díra and not been resumed. When questioned, one of the camera operators said circa half the equipment was gone, the other half no longer working. The chance of going back on air for the remainder of today's half-hour slot was effectively zero. Besides, communications with the control room had broken down. Nothing on any of the channels, and they couldn't get through on their phones either. The crew were all technical people with practical temperaments, so they decided to call it a day and check out Frikadellen village. See what meal deals they had on. 'Well, enjoy,' I said, less than impressed.

At this point, Drew and I started to pay attention to the particular nature of the re-materialised ground underneath. This was no longer the overgrown, rain-soaked ex-playing-field we'd got used to, but a soft and transparent surface. Beneath, an entire stadium not unlike the one we were in was discernible, imperfectly mirrored. On closer inspection and a fair amount of deliberation – 'is it?', 'it can't be', 'but it is!' – we established that this there underneath was the stadium we'd just left, the real Prokletý Field, upside down. In its regular place towards the east, the scoreboard projected downwards from our current POV. Six minutes and twenty-two seconds were left on it, counting down from the original ten. Not your regular ten, as it'd turn out——.

A short distance away, Malachi Hölderlin sat on the empty plinth, hairpins in mouth, redoing her chaos bun. Neither her first-ever trip through červí díra, nor the unfamiliar reality she found herself in, had changed her opinion of me. Seeing me looking at her, she gave me the backwards v-sign: up yours, Corey Fah. She was as determined as ever to ensure I would get what I had coming, she told me so in no uncertain terms. She might have relinquished her Kalashnikov, for Drew, but not her resentment towards me. 'See this?' she called, pointing down. As far as Malachi was concerned, the semi-automatic had been mere extra, mere fronting, a plaything, the warm-up to the main act. Her principal weapon had been the scoreboard all along, counting down what was left of me and my chances. 'Six minutes to go. See, Corey Fah?' Even here — whatever 'here' would turn out to be — the clock was still ticking, she was pleased to see.

'I was meant to have a whole year,' I protested.

But I didn't. Know why? Malachi had expedited my endpoint. She might as well own up to the fact that, early morning before today's show — if 'today' was still a relevant signifier — she'd secretly crept into the stadium, past one underpaid hence indifferent security guard. She'd crawled like invisible snake in the grass avoiding CCTV cameras. She'd made her way to the scoreboard undetected and scaled the unreasonably high scaffold it'd been mounted to. She'd interfered with the basic algorithm, and taken it all the way down from nine or ten months, several thousands of hours, to just twelve. That'd been eleven hours fifty-four minutes ago. Fifty-five. Tick tock. By the way, did either of us know how we'd get back to the other side? Drew?

We just left her there. I, for one, wasn't inclined to spend my final minutes with Malachi Hölderlin, if that'd really be it. I'd spend them with Drew, provided they'd have me. Walking, I tested my theory on them, about the redistribution of cultural capital leading to irregularities in the space-time continuum, affecting disadvantaged prize recipients disproportionately. What you think. Drew was all for it. Thought it made sense. But what, Corey, if anything, did that mean for us. Where were we. What was this place. If reality was beneath us, were we in an upside-down world? If it was, how *would* we get back — Malachi had a point. Drew stopped and probed the soft but resilient ground with their foot. Evidently, uber červí díra had closed good.

We stopped in front of a one-to-one replica of the Kalapács Road studio flat Sean St Orton had shared with his lover in '67. This version was drowning in blood. A see-through Plexiglas wall had been erected across the entire front of the scenery to contain circa twenty centimetres and rising of red sludge. Regardless, the flat was packed with people. The Social Evils prize coordinator was there. Substack subscribers I'd deserted were socialising with friends I'd lost touch with since my win and its repercussions had been preoccupying me. A banner had been put up on the wall, CONGRATULATIONS, COREY FAH! WE ARE PROUD OF

YOU, covering the peculiar sixties montage, and even a buffet had been laid out on a trestle table. No cucumber far and wide, I just knew. 'No one in the real world has thrown me a winner party,' I complained to Drew. What if this was the good place. Drew thought this overly optimistic. A look at the big scoreboard beneath confirmed we had three minutes and thirteen seconds left. There were further indications that all wasn't well: the waiter by the buffet looked uncannily like the prize coordinator. So did the technician setting up the smoke machine, though she was wearing a fake moustache. Malachi's mum was flirting with, of all people, the prize coordinator, and just beyond the stage set, near a door to the left, the prize coordinator was cutting wildflowers – to be arranged into my winner bouquet, by the prize coordinator. Towards the right of the flat, a small stage had been set up with a mic and a cheap PA, which, given the wet conditions, seemed ill-advised from an electrical-safety point of view. Just then, the Social Evils prize coordinator climbed up the couple of steps leading onto the stage. She went up to the microphone, testing, one. Nothing. Tap tap. Testing, testing. Nothing still. Can someone fix the PA? A sound technician who was the prize coordinator in Adidas Trophy hi-tops, a trucker cap and a bottle-opener keyring signalled ok. He'd take care of it. No problemo. PA just needed to be plugged in. With great determination, he waded through the floodwater towards the main plug in the wall, located right next to the trestle table, beneath the second U of WE ARE PROUD OF YOU. 'No!' I called. 'Don't do it!' Nobody heard, nor saw me. I ran towards the stage set and banged against the Plexiglas wall. Six seconds left on the scoreboard below. Five seconds. Four seconds. Three. I watched the sound technician bend down, fish for the plug of his amplifier in the murky liquid, find it and lift it. With one second left on the scoreboard, he pushed the plug straight into the electric socket——.

I wasn't dead. Didn't know about everyone else, but I could confirm, I hadn't been effaced from the Earth at this point. My time had yet to run out – *again*, as it'd turn out. I found myself in the upside-down stadium still, but it'd changed once more. In an audacious land grab, Frikadellen village had expanded from the north side, colonising the stands in every direction, as well as the playing field. One pink-brown outlet after the other, I myself was working in one. In too-short uniform trousers, matching t-shirt and cap, I was a version of myself who'd never written a book in their life. Didn't know how I knew, I just did. On the shelf above my cooking station was a radio alarm clock, a scoreboard proxy, showing nine minutes and forty-five seconds, counting down. I didn't have time to reflect on the implications of any of it. Matter of fact, I was on the phone to Frikadellen management. I regretted having to inform them that the meat supply had dropped off, meaning I wouldn't be able to meet my sales target. Sort it out, I demanded. Or else I'll lose customers.

Meanwhile, in the kiosk directly adjacent to mine, False Widower was serving frikadellen to the TBC crew as if there were no tomorrow. At this rate, he'd end up taking home a decent wage plus bonus. I couldn't believe he was still with the company eighty-two years down the line — not that historical continuity seemed to apply in the upside-down territory. But False Widower didn't just staff the kiosk to my left. As far as I could ascertain from my vantage point, he was also in the one to my right, and the one further along, and the one further along. Despite the fierce competition, a customer came up to *my* counter, ordering a frikadelle, rare, no mustard please. It was the Social Evils prize coordinator. She didn't recognise me. Had never met me in her life. Didn't see me, even, I was a mere extension of herself, reduced to a service provider. 'Sorry, I'm experiencing supply shortages,' I said. 'I ran out of mincemeat.' Overhearing this, False Widower to the left jumped at the chance to hike his bonus. How could he help, he shouted. He had all the juicy burgers the prize coordinator could wish for right here, rare, medium and very well done.

Preparing her order, False Widower spun the prize coordinator a story, telling her he was a rhetorician, a writer, a novelist, actually, one of the best in the upside-down realm. 'Watch this space,' he said. 'Watch your favourite publisher's future list, I'll be on it. Watch the bestseller charts, I'll be topping them.' In reality, False Widower had never written a book in his life, he never would. But, taken in, the prize coordinator said she looked forward to working with him in the very near future. Did he know, the Social Evils judging committee consisted of seven identical stags this coming year. The Great Prince-boss of the Fast-Food Restaurant was literally everyone on the judging panel. As part of their new employee reward scheme, Frikadellen, Best in Town would see to their own getting the recognition they deserved, even if they didn't. Such an ethical company, the prize coordinator concluded, biting into her burger. I was watching my radio alarm clock count down the remaining seconds, which I experienced as a relief.

This time round, I found myself in a TBC dressing room in the Gheto Attentat part of town, the upside-down version. Sean St Orton had never existed. I, *I*, was and had been the presenter of *Corey Fah Does Social Mobility*, a show without history. Nothing to do with the fact that each alternate reality lasted no more than ten minutes, apparently, nor Sean's death in '67 – just normal erasure. The world moved on at lightning speed, time waits for no man, et cetera, we did not give a fuck about those who'd come before in the international capital during this distinct era. Also, Drew wasn't here. Not in the dressing room, nor at home in Sociální Estate. They'd left me ages ago. TBC director burst in, asking, what's going on, Corey. Was I depressed, again? We'd go live in four minutes and I wasn't even dressed! Couldn't I find my boxing shorts in this tip? 'Get with the programme, Corey. People depending on you.' Director left the door to the dressing room open as he walked off, expecting me to follow him, stat. But I lay back on my sofa and stared at the ceiling for what felt like an age. Drei Sekunden, zwei Sekunden, eine Sekunde, null.

Drew! Oh thank god, Drew. We were back in the stadium, same set-up as when we'd first landed in the upside-down. Sociální Estate over there, and Frikadellen village, neatly contained on the north side of the stands. Couldn't see Malachi, though. Just Drew, sitting right next to me on the see-through ground, saying, 'We are caught in some time loop, or something.'

You too? I hadn't known what Drew's last couple of loops had been like, they had not been in mine. 'I was flipping burgers, Drew,' I reported. 'What about you?'

Didn't matter. Drew didn't care who'd been in whose time loop or not, nor who'd been flipping what. All they wanted to know was, how would we get out. A quick check confirmed that the scoreboard beneath showed nine minutes and two seconds – again. 'Looks like a kink in the countdown,' Drew said, 'possibly as a result of freak lightning strike.'

I didn't disagree. How will we stop it, though.

'Think,' Drew said. 'Historically, every time loop ever ended with the main character getting something right they'd previously got wrong, otherwise what would be the point. So, Corey. Over to you.' Clearly, I was the main character, everyone else a sidekick in my universe.

Allusion to my mild egocentrism, purely survival-based, but I allowed it. Could I have done anything differently? Could I? I didn't think so. I'd tried everything to get this trophy, and that's *after* it'd been awarded to me. When that'd turned into a lost cause, I'd let go and had moved into tv. Things between Drew and myself had deteriorated as a consequence, fine, but there was hope: they'd just shown they were still in the habit of rescuing me in the right-way-up world, which was reassuring.

Drew said that I wasn't addressing my failure to accept Bambi Pavok as my own, nor the role I'd played in his downfall. Or Sean St Orton, the role I'd played in *his* downfall. Fumper, Malachi, they'd all gone down because of me. What about landing us, not just in the upside-down world with little hope of returning, but inside a time loop. Was I sure I wouldn't do anything differently?

I didn't see it, still. If getting out of the time loop depended on me having a major insight, and adjusting my actions accordingly, I didn't fancy our chances. Was true I was stubborn, but also realistic and aware of the limitations of my personal agency.

'Even if I wanted to,' I said to Drew. Strictly speaking, the loops weren't even loops in this instance. If events were repeating themselves like in a classic time-loop set-up, we could identify patterns, work out how to disrupt or control them, and, eventually, based on what we'd learnt, force a different, more positive outcome, or not. But where we were at, every ten-minute period was entirely different from the one before. Nothing repeated itself. No learning opportunities and no second chances. I didn't know about Drew, but every ten minutes, I had another curveball thrown at me, travelling along a different trajectory, with a different spin. All I could ever excel at was reacting, crisis-managing and practising damage control. The best we could hope for was to be in the same time loop at the same time, so we could react together. Five seconds, four seconds, three seconds, two. We'd spent the entire ten minutes talking.

Just me this time. No Drew. When I say 'just' me——. Disconcertingly, I was in a crowd of myself, that is, various versions of myself from various historical junctures. I was — *we were* — filling the entire stadium, lined up like an infinitely detailed development study. There I was at nineteen, in light blue shorts and a red-brown t-shirt from the charity shop. More holes in my slip-on trainers than you'd care to imagine. I'd lived in the international capital for four years at this point, and I was about to meet Drew. I was looking a little forlorn, I have to say, but ok, I was doing it, I was staying alive by any means necessary. Here was me at thirty-two, refusing entry to the bailiffs again. Silver necklace with the conifer pendant on me, which I'd go on to lose the following year. DIY bowl haircut, not my best. Not even top ten. Resolute though, shutting the front door into the bailiffs' faces like I knew was my right. Drew would be so pissed with me later that night, finding out I'd not paid the council tax bill — again. Oh no — me in the public library. Lots of mes, ages twenty-five til thirty-five, studying hundreds of books of literature and philosophy, self-educating like no one was watching, cos, matter of fact, no one was. Blunt pencil in hand, marking mind-blowing passages with delicate crosses. I was reading as if my life depended on it, and it did, it did. None of my former selves were interacting with each other, which seemed sad from my current perspective. Nor did I feel a particular urge to go up and talk to any of them. They, *we*, seemed hugely preoccupied – absorbed in, if not consumed by, life. Shockingly, and I barely dare say it, the younger I got, the more I looked like Bambi Pavok. Here was me aged sixteen, completely alone in the capital. Four sets of eyes still intact, and believe, I needed them – there were perils around every corner. I'd just about made up my mind to go talk to the little one, when, four, three, two, I was gone.

My mother was alive in this next one. Ten minutes. I got ten complicated minutes.

Oh no. Not again. I thought I'd got away with it, but in this latest loop, I was forced to confront two further versions of my historical self. I experienced these encounters – this particular loop with its particular properties – as regular memories so I'll recount them straight: when first I arrived in the capital in '99, I hung upside-down under the roof of a bike shelter outside the international bus station for several days, unwilling to move. Environmental pressures or internal forces, I'll never know which, led me to embark on a process of assimilation at once: by day three, I'd lost two of my legs – they fell off almost casually, without fanfare. By day four, I'd discarded another one, which, while it pleased me, rendered me incapable of sustaining the traction required to stay in my safe place. I lost my hold and fell head-first into the bike rack underneath. Give it another couple of days, during which I just lay there, and I was two-legged – two-*armed* and two-legged, to be precise. On day seven, I watched one of the limbs I'd shed – curled up, not looking like much – get picked up by the rotating brushes of a mechanical road sweeper. I took this as a sign to gather myself together, get up and get a life. I was fifteen. Other aspects of my assimilation were harder to come by: there I was at age twenty-one – in familiar light blue shorts, red-brown t-shirt on the floor, threadbare by now – in the windowless room Drew and I shared in a flat in the east of the capital. I was twisting my neck, self-consciously examining the remaining white flecks on my back in the mirror. They'd faded, but, squinting, I could confirm that they hadn't disappeared. At the time, Drew tended to say they were fond of my flecks which made me suspect that they, Drew, had a fetish rather than e.g. love. But they didn't, have a fetish, they liked me, was all there was to it.

00:10:00. I recognised a scene from my relatively recent past in the right-way-up world. I sat on the sofa in our apartment, next to Drew. *St Orton Gets to the Bottom of It* was on, Drew glued to the tv. I watched some of it, mainly watched Drew emote, but I also had my laptop with me, half a novel on it. Could've been any afternoon in the three, four years leading up to the award. I thought about putting the laptop away, might as well. Might as well never write the book that'd won me the prize in the first place. When Drew had said to do one thing differently; to not do the thing that had led us here——. There hadn't been 'one thing', I'd said. Besides, they hadn't been things that I'd done, or could undo. But what if there was. Drew from the recent past laughed, 'Go on, Sean! Get to the bottom of it!' The show was in its heyday, and us, we were just us being us. Life was good, by and large. And yet, I couldn't do it, meaning I couldn't *not* do it. I couldn't just leave it be. It would have felt like a refusal of life itself. So I wrote, for ten minutes, while on tv, Sean failed to get to the bottom of anything.

Talking time in reverse Prokletý Fields stadium. Drew and I were in what I'd started referring to as the A-loop, the one that felt most like my actual life in my actual timeline. The one with a sense of continuity. The one where a narrative could build and develop; where plans could be made. Malachi Hölderlin was there too. She seemed oddly relieved to see us. 'Where are you when you're not in my loop,' I asked her. Yeah no, if she wasn't here in the A-loop with us, she was caught in what seemed like her future. Always solo, and always in the exact same setting: the white-tiled bathroom in her mother's apartment in Florida Rot. Nothing ever happened, or it hadn't so far, it didn't seem like her future was very eventful, to say the least. In the earlier loops, she'd gone round the apartment and established that mother was gone. She could tell from the fact that her,

Malachi's, belongings had been moved into the main bedroom, and the absence of cigarette smoke. Behind the apartment block, the swamp had been drained and turned into a construction site. They were building a corporate office building, or an industrial estate, or an amusement park, was hard to tell the difference at this stage. In more recent loops, she'd no longer bothered exploring. She'd just sat in the bathroom, waiting, for what, she didn't know. Fumper to re-emerge through the drain of the washbasin? Confirmation that his death had been avenged? Well, it hadn't, been avenged, Corey Fah, looking at you, looking so lively. Thing was, Malachi didn't care anymore. It had all been so long ago. So many ten-minute periods had passed, she'd lost track. Her future seemed pointless to the extent that it scared her. Anyway, pleased to see us. A-loop was a highlight in what felt like forever.

First time I felt sorry for the kid. What chance had she ever had.

How we gonna get back to the right-way-up world, though. Aware of the time constraints, six minutes and counting, Drew was keen to focus the conversation. How we gonna break out of this loop, what with Corey Fah unrepentant. They gave me a look. What if červí díra had never opened, Drew suddenly said. What if lightning hadn't struck, jinxing the scoreboard. We wouldn't have ended up in the upside-down, replete with the symptoms of timeline collapse. And we wouldn't be trapped in this loop, either.

Drew's speculations gave me an idea. What if I made sure the trophy would not be reteleported today. What if, at a pivotal point in the past, I asked for it to be taken, not to Prokletý Field, but to Florida Rot instead. Not teleported. *Taken*. Was my stupid award, I could do with it what I wanted, at least in theory. And I wanted it in Malachi's future. Every young person needed at least one thing to look forward to, otherwise what would be the point of living. Despite herself, Malachi's ears pricked up, I could tell.

'What if we prevent červí díra from opening, lightning from striking, find ourselves back in the right-way-up world and out of the time loop, and find that you, Corey, have ten unique minutes left on your clock,' Drew said.

They had a point, I had to admit.

'I know how to stop the countdown,' Malachi said. If she'd been able to speed it up, she could stop it. She'd figured out the scoreboard's workings when she meddled with it, earlier this, had it really been this, morning. A thousand time loops ago. Once we were back in right-way-up Prokletý Field, she'd go up the scaffold and fix it.

We'd managed to get Malachi on board. Who'd have thought.

'Ok, Corey,' Drew said. 'Do what you have to do.' They looked at me affectionately, impressed by my self-sacrificing gesture, perhaps.

Was a matter of staying alert. Of waiting for the right opportunity, then acting on it. Forty or fifty hugely variant loops down the line, I finally found myself in a set-up I thought I could manipulate for my purposes. I encountered myself round the time I first went on *St Orton Gets to the Bottom of It*, or just before, at Koszmar Circus, of all places. The bandstand had been turned on its head, balancing on the apex of its pyramid-shaped roof. The hydrangea and dog rose were heaving with bunnies multiplying at a supernatural rate. Striped skunks with little antlers were running in circles. My self from eight weeks ago looked as out of sorts as I felt, nothing major, just didn't know where to look with all the activity going on. Cute, though, how I was thrilled to see me. A little freaked, perhaps, but mostly elated. So I took my marginally younger self aside and had a word. I retained at least some of what I told me. Despite famously having trust issues with everyone else, I trusted myself implicitly. I agreed to go along with my proposition. I called the Social Evils prize coordinator while I waited, just like I'd asked me to. What's more, I delivered my request with unprecedented élan and entitlement – there being two of us worked wonders for my confidence. I asked that my trophy should be, not teleported, but personally taken, to Flat 13, Florida Rot apartment block, not now, but in twenty years' time, 2044, for the attention of one Malachi Hölderlin. M, A, L, A, C for catastrophe, H for hyperbole, I for it isn't so bad. Until that time, the trophy was to be kept under lock and key. Bury it, not my concern. Further, I instructed the prize coordinator to ignore any future instructions that might be diverging, even if they came from myself. To my surprise, the prize coordinator agreed. (What a difference delivery makes.) One caveat——. 'Giving Mallory, Malachi, the trophy won't mean she'll actually win the award,' the prize coordinator explained. That's ok, I replied. Winning the award hadn't meant I'd got given the trophy, either. We left it at that.

00:10:00 again. OMG. Drew? You see this? It worked! Prize coordinator had stayed true to her word. The trophy had not been reteleported today. In fact, there wasn't a sign of it, anywhere. We found ourselves back in right-way-up Prokletý Field. The scoreboard was towering above us, and the countdown was going down from ten minutes, taking a victory lap, so to speak. None of the strange sceneries and studio remakes remained – just the empty stands of a stadium in ruins, the regular wild meadow, the grey leather swivel chairs, and the one Frikadellen kiosk, consider it a warning. No person was represented more than once. Realising where she was, Malachi asked if she should get to it: 00:09:14. 'What if we just let it run,' I mooted. 'Let's take our chances. What's the worst that can happen.' Drew objected vehemently. They'd rather not know.

We watched Malachi go over and climb up the scaffold, screwdriver between her teeth. She'd left her gym bag with us, which I'd noticed had been empty since she'd pulled out her semi-automatic. But today, thousands of pages of, what, unusual writing spilled out. During thousands of ten-minute time loops, rather than wait, Malachi had got to work. She must've sat in that cold windowless bathroom that was her future and come up with this wonder, knowing that the prize coordinator, and also her day, would eventually come. Perhaps we'd been sidekicks in *her* universe all along.

The countdown stopped with a minute to go. 'Let's go home, Corey,' Drew said, 'Sociální Estate.' I looked at them – the one person who'd taught me, was teaching me, how to love on a daily basis. The one person who'd stuck with me, who I'd stuck with, and who allowed me, encouraged me, even, to change and become who I was or could be, for better or worse. 'Yes,' I replied, 'let's go home.' I picked up one of the pink plastic seats that lay in the grass, as a souvenir. I'd come to think of a souvenir as preferable, perhaps, to a trophy. I'd miss my career in tv which I was starting to accept would not come to fruition. Most of all, I'd miss

Bambi Pavok. I regretted I hadn't got to encounter him in any of the countless loops I'd gone through to get to this point, and it wasn't like I hadn't been looking. He'd been conspicuous by his absence. Really, though, I, Corey Fah, would be alright. That mouthpart I'd been hiding behind my tongue for so long, that had always been there, I relaxed it, I let it come out, dangerously, but candidly, honestly.

The following have been put to work in this novel:

Walt Disney – *Bambi*, 1942.
Nicole Eisenman – *Bambi Gregor*, India ink on paper, 1993.
John Lahr – *Prick Up Your Ears*, 1978.

Acknowledgements

Thanks to Hamish Hamilton and Penguin Books, especially Simon Prosser for editorial vision and being an agent of progress.

Thanks to Tracy Bohan from The Wylie Agency.

Thanks to Graywolf Press, especially Anni Liu and Yuka Igarashi, for publishing me in the US.

Thanks to the Goldsmiths Prize and those who conceived of it and run it: Tim Parnell and Livia Franchini. Winning in 2021 – as a writer lacking the structural privileges related to class, native status and cisgender heteronormativity – has made a significant difference to my practical circumstances. Thanks to the 2021 judges Kamila Shamsie, Nell Stevens, Johanna Thomas-Corr and Fred D'Aguiar.

Thanks to Linda Stupart for the glorious cover art.

Thanks to Peninsula Press, especially Sam Fisher.

Thanks to Dostoyevsky Wannabe.

Thanks to the queer, trans, black, POC and working-class writers showing us how it's done. Thanks to our readers and allies.

For Lisa Blackman.

ISABEL WAIDNER is a writer based in London. They are the author of *Sterling Karat Gold*, *We Are Made of Diamond Stuff*, and *Gaudy Bauble*. They are the winner of the 2021 Goldsmiths Prize and were shortlisted for the Goldsmiths Prize in 2019, the Orwell Prize for Political Fiction in 2022, and the Republic of Consciousness Prize in 2018, 2020, and 2022. They are a cofounder of the event series "Queers Read This" at the Institute of Contemporary Arts and they are an academic in the School of English and Drama at Queen Mary University of London.

The text of *Corey Fah Does Social Mobility*
is set in Fournier MT Std.
Typesetting by Jouve (UK).
Manufactured by Versa Press on acid-free,
30 percent postconsumer wastepaper.